The Holy Babble

Also by Dominic Kirwan and published by Ginninderra Press
Miracles Become Monsters
Put a Smile On That Face
Where Words Go When They Die

Dominic Kirwan

The Holy Babble

Thank you to Bridget Kirwan for help with the cover.

Thank you to Stephen Matthews. Stephen took a chance on me, helped me realise my dreams and gave my life a passionate purpose that continues to this day. Words cannot express my gratitude.

The Holy Babble
ISBN 978 1 76041 758 1
Copyright © text Dominic Kirwan 2019
Cover painting: *The Holy Babble* by Kim Loudon

First published 2019 by
GINNINDERRA PRESS
PO Box 3461 Port Adelaide 5015
www.ginninderrapress.com.au

Contents

Prologue　　7

The Tower of Babble　　9

Other People's Knickers　　20

Pewter Jesus　　26

Secret Santa　　34

The Holy Babble　　39

A Public Disturbance　　53

If You Are Reading This, I Am Already Dead　　58

Stranger　　67

Just Visiting　　92

Magpies　　100

Fans　　110

Carl　　127

The Donkey and the Pigeon (A Love Story)　　132

The Scribe　　137

The Wild and Unpredictable Sea　　150

The Night Inside the Day　　162

I had known loneliness before, and emptiness upon the moor, but I
had never been a NOTHING, a nothing floating on a nothing,
known by nothing, lonelier and colder than the space between the
stars. It was more frightening than being dead.
– Peter Carey

Prologue

Welcome to Moralpanik. Put your feet up. Make yourself at home.

Before we begin, allow me point out the obvious: you are not alone. There are others here too, hiding, waiting. When they gave up on their dreams, when they realised that their conception of the real world no longer had a need for them; they were drawn here: drunks and junkies and brain-fried hippies, the mentally ill and the abused, murderers and perverts, monsters and fuck-ups and super-duper-heroes, the delusional and the emotionally disturbed, predatory dreamers and masochists and Christian atheists. They all came here to disappear, for just a little while, and soon found that they could not leave. Those who have always lived here are hiding too. From exactly what, they cannot say. Perhaps if they could say anything at all, it would be to deny that it has anything to do with denial whatsoever.

So, let's get this merrymaking started, shall we?

Every perversion is welcome, every kinky urge and its action celebrated. Secrets here are embodied by other secrets, darkening the already suspiciously moist, shadowy walls of the fictional mind. Secrets are like that: they inform one another as they multiply, just like the secrets inside of us. Suicide is a popular last resort here. It is the ultimate holiday. The cemeteries are crammed with faceless tombstones. Moralpanik graves entertain imaginary mourners, and they are without flowers and without names.

There is something otherworldly about Moralpanik City. Its winding streets seem to lead nowhere except back to the beginning. Something sinister lurks beneath this strange city's sneering veneer. There are real reasons for this and there are real answers. But nobody can verify them; nobody can tell you why or when or how, and this is probably because nobody really knows.

Probably.

In any case, brace yourself for a most beguiling journey, Dear Traveller. And try to remember, no matter how ludicrous and macabre the ride, if you keep one hand on the asylum wall, you may just find your way out of the labyrinth. But will you emerge unscathed?

That, I'm afraid, remains to be seen.

The Tower of Babble

Two regular-looking guys with identical haircuts and bland faces and no outstanding or extraordinary features whatsoever, sit chained by their ankles to cubicles. In front of each of the men there is a rudimentary computer and a keyboard. This is the seventy-seventh floor of the Tower of Babble. The Tower of Babble is the main publishing company in Moralpanik City and its floors reach unfathomably high into the stratosphere.

One of them turns to the other and says, 'Psssst… Hey, what's your name?'

The other looks up from the computer keyboard he has been typing onto and says, 'I don't remember. What's yours?'

'I'm not certain I have a name.'

'Why do you think that is?'

'Only important people have names.'

This entire floor of the Tower of Babble is filled with a lot of similarly unremarkable people, chained to cubicles and typing furiously away. The enchained writers are not all bland and male, however. There are women and children and monkeys and midgets and a guy who stands out simply because he only has one arm. He types very slowly of course but he hopes to get promoted, just like everyone else. He doesn't know his name either, despite being different, and you'd think therefore interesting enough to have one.

One of the bland men says to the other, 'What are we supposed to be writing?'

'I'm not certain exactly,' replies the other in a hushed tone, 'but I hear if it's interesting enough it may find its way into *The Holy Babble*.'

'Who decides whether it will make it?'

'There's a guy upstairs, on the top floor. He decides.'

'Who is he?'

'I have no idea, but I used to sit next to a monkey who told me that we're all characters in his book. Weird theory, but you must remember he was a monkey. They think different to us. The monkey didn't have a name either. I don't know how he knew this stuff, but he seemed to believe it was true.'

'So, the guy upstairs is just ripping off stories from nameless guys like us and monkeys and who knows who else on the other floors, and he expects us to just keep submitting shit for nothing? That sounds fucked.'

'I suppose it is,' says the other plain man, 'but if we don't keep writing he'll get rid of us.'

'How will he do that?'

'He kills us off, like in a book, except we're not important enough to warrant a significant death, so we end up as statistics. You know, just another one of thousands caught in a fire on the sixty-eighth floor that never makes it out alive, a random unremarkable disaster with nameless victims. I think if we write something that he deems worthy of the book we're writing for him, we go up a few floors and get a nicer cubicle and they unchain you now and then so you can go to the toilet occasionally…even have a smoke and a cup of tea.'

'That sounds really nice. I think I'll try and write something catered to *The Holy Babble*. How about you, ummm…what did you say your name was?'

'I don't know.'

'Oh yeah. Come to think of it neither do I. I like your haircut by the way.'

'Thanks. I like yours too.'

The two men go back to typing away on their computer keyboards.

After a while one of them stops – it doesn't matter which one because they are so remarkably similar – and says, 'Come to think of it,

I did write something once that was almost accepted. They sent me up from the thirty-second floor to this one and I got an email that said the story showed misguided promise.'

'What's it like on the thirty-second floor?'

'Fairly unremarkable. It looks just like this one except they chain both ankles instead of one. Oh, and the Catering Reptiles don't come around with food for us every five hours like they do on this floor.'

'They starve you? That's horrifying,' gasps the other man in an animated but nonetheless bland manner.

'No…not exactly. They hook you up to a drip. Slot it right into the tip of the base of your spine and it keeps you alive. I think they fill the fluid bag with caffeine to keep you buzzed and to make you write faster. I'm not certain what else was in the fluid but I couldn't get any sleep at all. One night while most of the other writers were snoozing, I wrote a story for submission that almost got into the book we're in… or at least the book that we're supposed to be writing for that lazy, megalomaniacal fucker on the top floor. I thought it was a stroke of genius personally, but it was deemed inappropriate. Still, I got the promotion and now I'm sitting pretty on the seventy-seventh floor.' The unremarkable man smiles blandly with a hint of fond reminiscence in his eyes.

'Wow. I can't even remember anything from a week ago. I just woke up here, chained to this cubicle,' says the other man.

'Oh, that sucks. Hey…um…Nice Haircut Guy, would you like to read the story that almost got me in the book? I saved it on file just before I got promoted and snuck it up here with me. I'm not supposed to have a copy but maybe it will give you an idea what the fucker upstairs is looking for. I don't know how many floors there are before you get to the top, but if you write something for the guy upstairs that he likes you'll go up, and from what I've experienced it only gets better. We might even end up with character names if we're good enough.'

The guy with the regular haircut hands a flash drive to the other unremarkable guy who says, 'Thanks, I'll have a read.' He plugs the small device into a port on his computer and a file name appears on the screen. He double clicks on it and begins to read.

*

I The Birth of Santa

At some unfathomable time in the distant past there lived a couple of regular working-class folks. Their names were Joe Claws and Marie Claws. They met when they were working at a toy factory on the outskirts of Moralpanik City. At first, they didn't like each other very much, but when they discovered they shared the same surname, they took an immediate and perhaps superficial interest in one another. Maybe they were related, they thought; how very beguiling. They considered it was indeed possible they were distant second cousins four or five times removed but found the uncanny fact that they shared the same name enough of an impetus to begin engaging in sexual relations.

Marie Claws soon fell pregnant even though, according to the doctors, Joe was sterile. It had always run rampant in his family history. Apparently, Joe's father had also been sterile and so had his grandfather and his father before him. In this way, Joe Claws viewed the fact that Marie was expecting their child to be a continuing version of the miracle of his own unexpected entrance into the world (and that of every other member of his born-against-all-odds family).

Every Claw child had entered the world in this way as far back as history had recorded: with a look of awe and amazement on the part of Mr Claws; a sly expression of relief on the face of the birth mother (hiding a sense of guilt in the face of her free-and-easy-with-her-sexuality approach to getting pregnant to a man who was shooting blanks); and the child, every time born into the world with a sneer of confusion and wonderment that it had made it into and then out of the womb of its mother at all.

So, to Mr Joe Claws everything was a miracle and so too was his and Marie's soon-to-be-born child. It was another immaculate conception in a long line of immaculate deceptions. The only one not convinced it was a miracle was Marie of course, but she wasn't letting on.

The main problem was that Marie and Joe were not yet married and both of their respective families shared the belief that it was not only a sin to copulate outside the bounds of holy matrimony, but that a fitting punishment for such a transgression was to be pelted with stones until dead.

Fearing retribution, the couple eloped. They were married by an Elvis impersonator in a dodgy casino and then promptly attempted to flee Moralpanik City. When they realised this was impossible – there was no escape from the city because there were no roads leading out of town, and there were no other cities that they were aware of to flee to – Joe and Marie (who was heavily pregnant by that time) merely moved to the other side of town.

One night, when their attempts to locate an inconspicuous hospital failed, they attempted to get a room at a motel. When they failed to procure a cheap enough room, they settled on an old barn that was more likely a garage for sick cars. Once inside, Marie, lying on a heap of straw that was more likely a small mountain of oily rags, gave birth to a baby boy. When he shot out of the womb, Joe and Marie were surprised to discover that the little boy already possessed a large snow-white plume of facial hair. He was plump with sparkling blue eyes and rosy-red cheeks.

Instead of crying, he laughed when he saw the look of horror on his father's face. 'Ho, ho, ho…' he rumbled merrily, pointing at his blushing mother Marie.

They called the boy child Santa and decided he was special, for not only was he fat and already amply bearded, but because Joe believed he was a miracle. He decided he would teach his son to make toys for other children, as they had done in the factory. Because he was born in such special circumstances, Joe believed it would break the curse of their low-income bracket and they would make money by celebrating their son's birthday every year on the same day. They would share the miracle of giving and receiving with the people of Moralpanik City while becoming immensely rich in the process. The best way to do this, Joe decided, was to spread the Good Word that Santa, his only son, was a magical toy-making prophet. Despite the ludicrous and arrogant disposition of Joe's ambitious plan, it came to fruition. Only not exactly in the manner Joe had dreamt.

As Santa grew to maturity, so did his giving reputation. The toys he made sold well at first and the people of Moralpanik embraced his mysterious repute. The rumours spread and, like Chinese whispers, became more and more fantastical. Apparently, he would visit the houses of children who had made it onto a mystical list dividing everyone into two categories – the Naughty and the Nice. Word of mouth spread that he lived somewhere very cold indeed. He flew on a sleigh with magical reindeer but once a year, his birthday, delivering his toys to the well behaved and deserving children of Moralpanik.

Unfortunately, this was all a load of horse shit. The real Santa Claws lived on his own by the age of thirty; had given up making his own toys because none of the toy factories would buy them any more, and instead lived a miserable and solitary alcoholic life. Watching on as the corporate toy companies, the super supermarkets and the infrastructure of Moralpanik's capitalist dream factory made billions of dollars every year, flogging off his image to parents who would in turn lie about his true activities and purpose to their children. Around that time of year, kids were better behaved. Parents brought a multitude of toys from stores such as Toys R Ploys and pretended to their children that Santa had magically broken into their houses in the middle of the night and left them there. Treasures wrapped in red and white festive paper with little notes from Santa to their nice children, written in what looked suspiciously like Mum or Dad's very own handwriting.

This really began to piss the real Santa off. How dare they exploit his image for their own financial gain! The real Santa Claws had become a bitter and twisted man who lusted for revenge. He realised he had become an imaginary simulacrum of a temporary lie told to children in order to keep the system cycling through a consumerist nightmarescape. The worst part was that even though the children loved their conception of Santa, when they were old enough it was revealed to have been a lie all along. It was a necessarily beautiful but nevertheless temporarily-temporary lie. Santa couldn't win.

It was around this time that Santa began to suspect that he did not exist at all. His superb but imaginary public image was ripped from the hearts and minds of children everywhere just when it looked like he might be real after all. The only one who knew the real Santa was Santa himself. Joe had given up on his son when his second run at toy-making faltered commercially, and Marie had long ago left her sterile husband for another sterile man to whom she was also mysteriously pregnant.

II Metamorphosis

It was all too much for Santa. The combination of alcohol, hallucinogens, crack cocaine, depression and stress brought about a terrible identity crisis in him. His mind split into many different fragments. Almost unconsciously, he began to formulate a second separate personality. He steadily became convinced that he was slowly evolving into a bunny rabbit. The metamorphosis in his mind soon began to literally inflict his actual physical body, creating a new and tangible anatomical reality. His snow-white beard receded and smooth fur spread across his body. His nose began to twitch uncontrollably and sprouted whiskers, and he felt ears, long floppy white ears growing from the back of his head. He hopped around town jiggling his new fluffy button tail and doing strange dances for awestruck families and children in the streets of Moralpanik. After a while, he decided to legally change his name to Bunny. As he paraded the streets, his reputation began to precede him; the newspapers and tabloids featured this strange rabbit-man more and more frequently. It was his second chance at life, a rebirth.

The real breakthrough came when he was at the Moralpanik Zoo one day. Bunny Claws – who was at the time entertaining a small rabble of enthralled children – felt that he badly needed to defecate. In fact, he needed to poop so badly he simply couldn't wait. Instead of racing off behind a tree or to the nearby public toilets, he dropped the contents of his bowels right there in front of all those children.

The look of horror on the faces of the impressionable youths was immediate and almost soul-destroying to the man who had grown quite fond of his new appearance and reputation. So, without skipping a beat, he scooped up the remarkably spherical turd and, holding it aloft, nervously proclaimed to those gathered, 'Look… I laid an egg!'

At first the crowd, who had now swelled in ranks to a few hundred, were not buying it. 'Look, the stupid bunny did a shit!' they crowed cruelly.

With all those eyes fixed firmly upon him, with the weight and significance of all that he had once been and who he had now become, spiralling out of control inside him, Bunny did the most desperate and potentially disgusting thing he could think of. He put the egg-shaped dump in his mouth and, although immediately reeling from the horrible taste of his own excrement, instead smiled widely and proclaimed, 'Mmmmmmm… Yum-yum-yummy… Chocolate!'

To his surprise, the crowd erupted into rapturous applause. Suddenly, the children all wanted a chocolate egg laid by the magical Bunny. This news spread like wildfire, and so did the demand for chocolate eggs. Some of the corporations approached Bunny, pleading with him to lay more so that they may line the shelves of their super supermarkets and cash in on the strange and magical craze. Bunny Claws refused, saying his eggs were not for sale and neither was his magic. Although, he did agree to allow them to mass produce chocolate eggs on the condition that he got a cut of the profits and a multimedia deal with the Fix-Sell Broadcasting Corporation. Bunny Claws appeared on many television shows and specials, preaching the value of chocolate eggs to the masses and hinting that he was indeed a Messiah trapped in the body of giant bunny rabbit. Eventually all the hype began to go to his head and he had yet another mental breakdown.

During this time, a rebel group of other much-smaller-and-infinitely-envious bunny rabbits started a petition to expose and ban the Bunny Man from television. They said he was a fraud and disputed his ability to lay eggs at all, let alone chocolate ones. The still spellbound and sugar-addicted public ignored this for a while, continuing to consume his endorsed chocolate products. Bunny Claws retreated from the television eye, ashamed of his lie yet still convinced of his divine nature. It seemed no different than when he was Santa Claws. The cycle continued despite his slowly crumbling sense of reality and guilt.

He shakily preached on hillsides to people who were more interested in seeing him lay a chocolate egg than absorbing the majesty of his transcendental insights. 'Love your chocolate as yourself,' he said to those who would gather. 'Love the Lord your Bunny with all your heart,' he also proclaimed.

III Crucifixion of the Bunny

Eventually, a particularly sneaky and cunning journalist who worked for a current affairs program that cut down tall poppies uncovered the truth. She procured a sample of one of the Bunny Messiah's public dumps before he could eat it and smile once again, proclaiming, 'Mmmmmmm…chocolate!' Instead she quickly called rabbit-shit on the whole façade. The ensuing television exposé was viewed in record numbers. The people cried out for blood. They wanted to crucify the shit-eating Bunny. There was a little resistance at first but soon the Bunny Man was forcibly removed from his rabbit-hole mansion and dragged up the side of a mountain carrying a wooden cross.

People lined the streets on all sides as the sick parade continued towards its inevitable conclusion. The Bunny Man was riveted to a crucifix, nails were driven through his paws and he was left there to die. Children threw chocolate eggs at him and ridiculed the Bunny.

After many hours writhing in pain, he was heard to call out, 'Father, why have you forsaken me? Was it because I never made any money selling my own toys?'

The Bunny Messiah died, right there on the cross.

An obnoxious child pierced his side with a makeshift toy spear and dark brown fluid trickled down the dead Bunny Messiah's leg. The child, a former disgruntled fan, was curious as to the nature of the dark ooze. So he ran his finger through it and held it to his lips. 'Mmmmm…yummy. It really is chocolate!' he exclaimed, and then promptly fainted, collapsing to the ground as the insulin levels in his body capsized in holy ecstasy.

With little fanfare, the Bunny Messiah was buried.

But days later his grave was found empty and the tombstone cracked in two. Some say it was the work of sugar-addicted grave robbers, hungry for his chocolate blood. Others say they even saw him in the following days, holes in his paws and still weeping dark chocolate. Consensus now is that the Bunny Man returned to a place in the sky where his sterile father Joe (who had killed himself shortly after Marie left him) was eagerly awaiting him to reconcile with his long-lost son and embrace him, proud of all that his son had accomplished, and for all the money he had inadvertently injected into the Moralpanik economy.

Indeed, some believe he will one day return to us. On the day of Reckoning he will come – to punish the naughty and reward the nice. Some say there is a place in the sky for those who lie to their children, giving them gifts from a magical Santa Claws on his immortal birthday and stuffing their faces with expensive chocolate eggs on the day he rose from the grave.

And yet there are some…some who believe none of it at all.

Amen.

*

The bland man with the regular haircut looks up from his computer screen, having finished reading the story that almost-but-not-quite made it into the book he may-or-may-not be in. He makes a copy of the file on his own computer, not intending to tell its author of the deliberate theft. 'Psssst… Hey! Regular guy,' he says.

The other blander than bland man cranes his neck around the side of his cubicle. 'Yeah…um, what's your name again?'

'I don't know…but that was really silly. I can see why the guy upstairs didn't accept it,' he says, not wanting to let on that parts of it really resonated with him.

'Oh, that's too bad. Why didn't you like it?'

'It's not that I hated it. It's just that I don't believe the guy upstairs would ever put it in a book.'

'Why not?'

'Nobody in their right mind would buy into that shit.'

'Oh, I suppose you're right,' the author of the just rubbished story says in a disappointed but nonetheless bland tone.

'I like your haircut, though,' the bland reader guy says, smiling grimly in self-satisfied consolation.

'Thanks, man. I like yours too.'

Other People's Knickers

The Collector peered through a crack in the fence. He stared longingly at the underwear on the neighbouring clothesline. He pushed his face into the wood and splinters ground into his cheek. A rush of excitement and nervous longing thrashed against his insides, making him feel dizzy, dirty. The clothes line swivelled in the wind, revolving like a fallen windmill, beckoning him.

He wore a pastel blue tracksuit, streamlined by two navy blue lines. The zipper was broken and the jacket awkwardly fastened together at a point just above his navel. There were grass stains on the knees and elbows of the outfit, evidence of the physical rigours of his trade. No amount of stain remover or soaking would remove them. To the Collector they were occupational scars, blemishes on his armour.

He pushed his face further into the eye hole and strained to see the back of the house. There was no sign of the Fat Lady. By his estimation, he guessed that she lived on her own. There were never any clothes but her own hanging on the line, and she rarely entertained guests. In her mid to late thirties, he watched her thick varicose ankles carry the weight of her enormous breasts and baskets of wet clothes across the yard every three or four days. She pegged bras, petticoats, summer dresses and those delightfully immense knickers to the line. The Collector could time her approach by the stuttering cough of the washing machine, the wretch and shudder of another dying spin cycle. He could not, however, predict exactly when she would take them down. This lent the raids on this line an element of danger, a risk factor. After years of experience at the game, building up his collection with professional finesse and cunning, he found that eventually everyone notices that their knickers are going missing. If the Fat Lady hadn't already, she would soon. The trick was to know when to move on. He should wait until nightfall; play it safe. That would be the sensible thing to do. But the chance she might take down her clothes before he took advantage of this small window of opportunity necessitated risk.

But why did he feel so nervous? After all, he'd done jobs just like this hundreds of times before. Hadn't he? Mental note: breathe deeply…focus…and stop shaking. He began to limber up, stretching his calf muscles, twirling his arms and wiggling his fingers, and then for the finale: ten feisty star jumps to get the blood pumping.

He removed a fence plank, which he had marked with a small white X, then the two on either side of it. Peeking through the gap, his eyes carefully scanned the landscape. The back door of the house was closed and the outside laundry, at the side of the patio, appeared to be empty. He leaped through the gap and launched into a lusty forward roll. Rising to his feet, he pinpointed the target: a pair of pink jumbo knickers that he had been eyeing off for a while. They had a frilly band of pink lace around the leg holes and a vast cotton seat. He guessed they were a size twenty or twenty-two and, taking the fancy lace design into account, this made them particularly rare. The brand he could not be sure of. One thing was for certain, though: knickers that big and with that workmanship could not be purchased locally, nor were they cheap. He wondered where they would fit in his collection. They could be a foreign prototype, and not easily classified.

If the Collector were asked to explain himself, what would he say? Firstly, he would stress that one does not find an original in the isles of a supermarket. One cannot purchase greatness. Then he would get that knowing smile on his face, like a crack in slow-drying plaster. Obviously, an undergarment of value must come from its source, its creator, but it is not stealable until it has been worn at least once, he would say.

The Collector rarely wore garments from his own collection. He had in the past, but not for reasons one might expect. He once tried on a yellow thong that he had stolen from a lady who perpetually sunbathed in her backyard, but only to see if they really were more comfortable than bike pants. Over the years, his curiosity for sexual titillation regarding his craft had played itself out. He did sniff his collectibles, but only to see if they needed rewashing. The aroma of unwashed knickers was not repulsive to him – he had done that for a while too – but a garment lasted longer if it was clean. Ingrained sweat and dirt led to bacteria and ultimately rot.

There was something about the ritual of theft that made his catches more interesting. He did study his victims, but only to establish patterns of behaviour that would assist him with the job, the panty raid. For some reason, though, he always remembered the former owner; certain physical traits remained etched in his memory. These recollections enhanced his fondness for certain catches, even if they were ordinary ones.

Those beauties would soon be his, the prize catch of his collection. He took two small steps to the right, cocked an eyebrow and steadily raised his hands into the air. He took a moment to calculate the distance and then threw himself into action, executing another perfect forward roll. When he stood up, he was directly behind a floral sheet and pleased to notice that it concealed him from the back of the house. If she were to look through the back door or window, he would be out of sight. He paused and sniffed at the air, licking his finger and holding it thoughtfully to the breeze. If the wind were to suddenly blow, his shoes would give away his position. So he made a grab for the knickers, removing them from the line with a dexterous snap of the wrist. The pegs popped into the air and one whistled past his ear. He had them, bingo; time to get out of there. Before he could move, though, he heard a dull squeal. The back door of the house swung open. He froze. A dry lump swelled in his throat, choking his resolve. A sudden gust of air lashed past and the clothes line began to turn again. If he didn't act, he'd be caught for certain. So he reached up and clasped the slowly turning line, bringing it to a halt just as the sheet whipped up in the wind, exposing him. Without thinking, he brought the pink jumbo knickers up to cover his mouth and nostrils, like a child caught in a game of hide and seek. He bit into the fabric and, on a reflex, inhaled. The knickers smelt strange, sickly, wet. The fumes went straight to his head.

The last thing he heard was a shriek of victorious laughter, and the words, 'Got Ya!'

Then the world disappeared.

When the Collector awoke, he found he was strapped to a sturdy wooden chair and unable to stand. His hands were bound with what felt like gaffer tape. His mouth was gagged with cloth and his ankles were strapped to the legs of the chair.

'Ah, so you're alive,' a voice said.

The Collector looked up to see the Fat Lady.

She smiled at him wickedly. 'I thought you might've overdosed!' she hissed. Her laughter, though, did not mirror the look in her eyes, which were dark and vengeful. She held a small, half empty bottle of clear liquid up to his eyes. 'This stuff didn't come with instructions, you know,' she guffawed.

The Fat Lady walked up behind him and gently stroked his hair. 'Knew I'd catch you eventually,' she said. 'Just needed the right cheese.'

She moved back to where he could see her. 'Got something for you, a present for a being a naughty mouse.' She playfully pinched his nostrils closed with two pink stubby fingers.

He shook his head violently, struggling to breathe. She let go and strutted into the next room. When she returned, she was wearing nothing except for a pair of men's white Y-fronts. They were far too small and stretched almost to the point of tearing. She began to dance; her enormous breasts jiggled across her belly. She swung her hips to the beat of silence and his throbbing heart.

She gestured at the underpants. 'These little babies are yours, you know,' she smirked, suggestively slapping her own behind. 'Got plenty more where these came from too,' she panted.

She sat on his lap, pinning him to the chair. She put her arm around his neck and wiggled to get comfortable. When she was settled, she pulled the gag from his mouth. He coughed hard, spraying the Fat Lady with his spittle. She held the gag aloft, opening it to reveal a pair of colossal pink knickers. She pointed to the tag, and the Collector's heart sank: Bonds. He'd been caught trying to steal a pair of Bond's knickers. How could he have been so stupid? The Fat Lady wiped the corners of his mouth with them and gently dabbed at his flowing tears. The Collector didn't know whether to feel comforted by her gesture, or whether to scream. But how would that sound? He'd pinched at least a dozen pairs of her underwear and she could probably prove it. If the cops searched his house, they'd find hundreds of pairs of other people's knickers. Carefully catalogued according to value, brand and size; meticulously shelved between sheets of tissue paper; each piece accompanied by notes explaining from where and whence they were stolen, and their relative and personal value to the Collector. No, if he screamed now, he'd be finished.

He wouldn't do it again. No, he'd be a good little mouse from now on, he'd promise her until he was blue in the face. But something deterred him, something he couldn't quite explain. It was a feeling of morbid curiosity, the wonder of not knowing what was going to happen next. Even if he convinced her how sorry he was, it wouldn't do him any good. The Fat Lady wasn't going to let him go.

She leaned into him and softly began to sing into his ear. 'Oh, Mickey you're so fine, you're so fine you blow my mind, hey, Mickey…' she chanted.

She reached behind him and, almost too conveniently, retrieved two white cheer leading pompoms. Bounding excitedly to her feet, her rolls of fat jiggled in crudely choreographed motion to the song.

The Collector knew it was all over, an inconvenient but inevitable ending. But then, his sense of impending doom segued into an eerie calm, the fear becoming familiar, almost comforting. He knew that he'd be caught eventually, that the darkness would chase him down.

What he didn't know was the Fat Lady's name, and whether, after she'd finished with him, she'd like to check out his collection. He also wondered if she did this often, and if so, what was her excuse?

The Fat Lady continued to dance for him, chanting the words of the song and pressing his face between her swinging breasts. The Collector tried to ignore her, to shut her out. This wasn't right. He was enjoying this far more than he ought. He closed his eyes and forced a smile, retreating into himself, taking solace in his besieged imagination.

For what he feared would be the last time, he pictured endless lines of knickers stretching out for as far as the eye could see, fluttering prettily in the summer breeze.

Pewter Jesus

The house barely stands upright. Like a decrepit old man who refuses to shuffle off his mortal coil, it is held together by dreams long past. A ramshackle structure with floorboards that creak like crooked vertebrae, its interior crawls with the ghosts of carnivorous rats and stinks of sweaty, fetid cheese. A tattered sprawl of classic Andy Warhol wallpaper covers the lounge room walls, and it is lathered in a greasy film of mould, cobwebs and dust. A pewter crucifix displaying a reluctantly suffering Christ hangs from a rusty nail protruding from the wall; it partially obscures one of Marilyn Monroe's wallpaper faces.

Jesus looks down upon his scantily clad body and yearns to adjust his loincloth. The sensation of longing is almost unbearable, the throes of martyrdom an unfortunate by-product of his immovable suffering. If he weren't so permanently moulded to his crucifix, he would like to tend to those unreachable itches. A small black spider dangles from a web growing from his smooth pewter cheek. Jesus speaks to it when he feels lonely, which is most of the time, but the spider rarely replies.

At the far end of the room there is a floral couch. A pattern of dull yellow sunflowers adorns its faded lining. Stuffing spews from holes in the chair, like emulsions of cotton wool lava from volcanic wounds.

Mary lies sprawled across the couch, naked except for a pair of laddered black stockings and a chaotic smear of eyeliner and lipstick. Beneath her tousled auburn fringe two bloodshot eyes strain to peer over her pregnant paunch. Her knees stand like two balding soldiers guarding either flank of her belly. She is experiencing contractions. 'It's probably a false alarm,' she thinks. She's had them before, and the baby isn't due for another three weeks yet.

Joseph has other ideas, he is positive this is IT.

The exact nature of Joseph's IT, however, is something Mary cannot quite fathom. He stands at the end of the couch, also naked except for a shiny red cape that is far too short and only half covers his pasty white buttocks. His smiling gob bobs up and down like a rotten apple in a bucket of dirty water. Mary marvels at his unbridled enthusiasm. His face beams like a fiendish sunrise, ascending from the horizon of her paunch.

Mary thinks Joseph is just Super.

Her preference, had she been afforded one, was to give birth to her first child in the relative comfort and safety of a hospital. Joseph had insisted otherwise, demanding the right to his own privacy at such an important event. It was all part of Joseph's master plan: the ritual of birth augmented by his own desire to wear, do and say exactly as he pleased.

'Doctors and nurses have their place,' he would exclaim, 'but not at my birth.'

Joseph's choice of words had sent a strange shudder through Mary. She wanted so badly to trust him but it wasn't easy sometimes.

The line between eccentricity and lunacy, in Joseph's case, simply does not exist. In the unlikely event that there is only one universe, Joseph is at its very centre. Wearing a jewelled crown, Superman outfit and shit-eating grin, he sits on his throne and waves royally at all those that look his way. An unrepentant megalomaniac with a penchant for the theatrical, he nevertheless has his charms. At least Mary thinks so. She finds that he makes her life more interesting, because she never can tell what he will do next.

'No need to worry,' Mary thinks. 'Everything always works out in the end…doesn't it?'

It should be noted at this point that, in terms of her relationship with Joseph, Mary doesn't necessarily have her finger on the pulse of reality. It should also be obvious that Joseph has no pulse, is not repulsed, and is very possibly pulsating. But in the here and now, Mary doesn't mind being sidelined by Joseph's antics. She is, however, beginning to regret not standing up for her right to a safe hospital delivery. Mary is not stupid; she's just careless, and more than a little naïve. She suspects Joseph merely wants to bask in the glory of his creation, without the possibility of snide laughter and the narrow mindedness of professionals. She is only partially correct in this assumption. Things of this nature are usually worse than one thinks and they seldom go to plan. For this reason and a few more unspeakable ones besides, Mary has decided she will play along with the game, for now.

Joseph's eyes crawl like flies, bulbous and insect like, all over Mary. His reassuring smile is gone. It has been replaced by something far more sinister: a morbid fascination with the contours and possibilities of her lower body. His fiendish giggle is frequently interrupted by awkward facial twitches. Mary has not seen Joseph this excited before. Every now and then, almost as a guilty afterthought, he nervously eyes the crucifix hanging on the wall. Joseph suspects that he is being watched, and he is correct in this assumption, as two beady pewter eyes follow his every movement.

From his place on the wall, Jesus looks on in disgust. He knows what Joseph is up to. He wants so desperately to intervene, to say, 'Oh devil of the seven deadly lusts, I cast thee out!' But his pewter lips are moulded shut. Besides, he isn't certain that he has the wording right.

Mary is also troubled. Joseph's erratic behaviour is beginning to alarm her. Perhaps it is merely the intensity of the contractions, she thinks. The unborn child has somehow found a knife and is running its sharp edge across the walls of her uterus. She winces in pain, cursing Joseph under her breath.

Joseph is either oblivious to her suffering or he has more important things to do. Holding his arms out in front of his chest, he pretends that he is flying. His little red cape flutters in the breeze that wafts through the open window. He affects exaggerated whooshing sounds, dipping and twirling across the room like a drunken dervish.

At the very beginning of their relationship, in the throes of passion, Joseph would cry out, 'Lois, oh Lois!' At first, Mary had been offended, figuring he was referring to an ex-girlfriend. But she didn't mention it, hoping that his feelings for this woman would eventually be eclipsed by their blossoming romance. When she eventually questioned him about it, Joseph became terribly embarrassed, pleading that he had no control over the outbursts. Mary became so incensed that one evening, after much deliberation, she stormed into the bedroom and sarcastically cried, 'Oh take me, Superman!' Joseph almost wet himself with glee, throwing his arms around her neck and weeping tears of joy. The very next day he went out and purchased a little red cape from a Toys R Ploys store. Unfortunately for Mary, he had worn it ever since. He even went so far as to wear the cape under his shirt when they went about town. The potential for public embarrassment was now manifold. Every telephone booth they passed in the street was a tempting prospect for Joseph, and Mary often had to physically drag him away, kicking and screaming like a child throwing a temper tantrum. The resultant sulking was almost as tragic. Mary often tried to picture him without the cape but found that she no longer could.

Mary thinks Joseph is just Super.

He hinted that he had something special in mind, but Mary can't imagine what it might be. Mary cares for Joseph, she really does. It's just that now she wants to throttle him, to pry his jelly white eyes out of their sockets. Instead, she digs her fingertips deep into the couch, tearing at the faded sunflowers, all the while imagining she is scratching the smile off his face.

'Help me,' she pleads silently, hoping her unborn child will hear.

Joseph's eyes have grown immeasurably and Mary is afraid they might leap from their sockets and smother her. She feels her unborn child gnawing on her umbilical cord, clamping its little gums into the lifeline, gripping the tender noose with two tiny pink fists in a calculated ploy to remain inside her.

Joseph's paranoia finally overcomes him. He dashes across the room and snatches the pewter crucifix from its place on the wall. Throwing it in the corner, he hastily covers it with a dirty dishcloth.

Jesus breathes a deep sigh of relief. The darkness provides welcome respite from the nightmare that is unfolding outside.

Now it is Marilyn's turn to watch, and she pouts suggestively, parading her immovable but sensual wallpaper lips in anticipation. Hopefully, something interesting will happen, she thinks. Usually anything worth seeing happens in the bedroom, at least that's what she suspects, and her mighty empire doesn't stretch quite that far. Sure, the little man on the pewter cross has the integrity, the respect, but Marilyn Monroe has the numbers. After all, in this room, she is everywhere, and Marilyn doesn't intend on missing a thing.

Joseph strives to impress Miss Monroe, fully aware that all her eyes are on him. Strutting like a puppet rooster, dancing like a horny marionette for a voyeuristic god. There was a time when Mary would have been insanely jealous. She would have wanted Joseph all to herself.

Mary used to think Joseph was Super. Now she isn't so sure.

Returning to the end of the couch, Joseph addresses the unborn child. 'This way, boy. Out of there now,' he says.

Leaning even closer so he can be heard, he shouts out directions. 'Claw your way out of there now, boy,' he says. 'This way, this way… you just follow my voice and I'll guide you.'

Joseph has disappeared. All Mary can feel are his warm irregular breaths on her crotch. He is growing impatient, muttering to the unborn child in a low sickly whisper.

Through Joseph's eyes, Mary's groin suddenly contorts, bending out of shape and defying rational form. The screen goes blank…silent. Particles of light disperse and then re-form, merging finally into something clear, something that wasn't there before. What appears to Joseph to be a mouth, with huge blabbering lips and crooked yellow teeth, has materialised between Mary's legs.

'Joseph? Come on doooowwwwnnnn!' it sneers. 'It's all right… I won't bite your head off.'

Joseph begins to wail hysterically at the newly shaped cavity.

Mary is now terrified. What is going on? Her eyes dart about the room, wildly searching for a convenient exit or escape clause. She feels like she cannot move. Why is that? There is an empty vase on a table near the wall. She could smash Joseph over the head with it, but she cannot quite reach that far. This is wrong, this is too much. Mary reels in panic.

Marilyn isn't impressed either. She wants to close her eyes but they are painted open.

It feels like the child inside Mary is driving the knife in deeper, carving unspeakable obscenities into the fragile tissue walls. The room is closing in around her. It too has become a womb, wet with the discordant echoes of their screaming.

Joseph wedges his skull between Mary's now tightly closed shins and pushes. 'If you won't come out, I'm comin' in,' he grunts.

If Joseph had any insight at this point, he would know that the exercise is mired in futility. His efforts are an unfortunate conglomeration of tired slapstick and the feeling of distress one experiences during constipation.

His feet scramble to grip the tatty linoleum floor but inevitably cannot.

[Cue canned laughter.]

He slips across the sweaty surface, giving the impression he is running on the spot.

[Cue canned laughter.]

He sprints frantically on an almost horizontal angle, desperate to force his way beyond Mary's snapped-shut thighs into what he thinks is heaven.

[Cue toilet bowl flushing.]

Joseph, it would seem, just wants to go home.

Finally, something inside Mary breaks; a series of synaptic impulses cascade into violent motion. She screams out loud, performing a blood-curdling rendition of the Lord's Prayer. Her muscles relent momentarily, as if weary from the struggle, then suddenly she pounces on her prey, crushing Joseph's ears to the sides of his head with her thighs, tightening her grip like a steel vice on a tomato. Joseph lets out a high-pitched squeal and bites deep into his own tongue. With a desperate spasm, he springs out of Mary's deadly grip and staggers back from the couch.

Marilyn is finding the entire spectacle to be an awful bore. It all seems so tedious and primitive, not to mention vulgar. Is there supposed to be a point to all this crap, she wonders? Is there a way out of this place?

Jesus lies perfectly still under the dishcloth and, strangely enough, he can't help but feel a little neglected. It isn't that he approves, not at all. He just feels that he's finally had it with the pose, the cross, and the whole damned icon thing. Being Jesus is highly overrated, he feels frustrated and alone. The best course of action is to ditch the holier than thou attitude for something more cutting edge, more now perhaps. Dying for everyone's sins is all well and good but being nailed to a cheap pewter crucifix for eternity is the worst kind of cliché. There's nothing remotely sexy about it, thinks Jesus, nor is it strictly necessary.

Joseph backs up to the wall and Marilyn's torn wallpaper lips press against his red-caped spine. Wiping the moisture from his eyes, his vision clears and he slowly absorbs the scene before him.

Mary is now propped up on her elbows, and the crazed look in her eyes suggests a deathly challenge. 'Yeah… bring it on, Superman,' she hisses.

Joseph knows where he wants to go. Nothing is going to stand in his way, least of all Mary and her impetuous child. Joseph thrusts his arms out in front of his chest once more, flicking his foot back and forth across the floor, snorting like a mad bull sizing up a matador.

Deep inside Mary, a boy child chuckles mischievously. He nuzzles his smooth contented face into the walls of an invitingly claustrophobic universe. One of his pink supple legs dangles down, guarding the exit. He flexes his little toes, poised to stomp on the intruder's head. It is a territorial gesture; the child is preparing for war.

Joseph lets out a maniacal battle cry. Lowering his head in a penetrative gesture, he charges full tilt towards Mary. Her legs kick out like powerfully coiled springs, connecting with his balding skull. Shattering his spirited onslaught and lifting him up off the floor, she sends Joseph reeling back across the room in an explosion of sweat and whip-lashed bone.

Once she has caught her breath, Mary picks herself up off the couch. The contractions are steadily receding. She slips on some underwear and a bra, her dress and shoes, and looks down at Joseph, curled up in a ball, rocking back and forth and sobbing into a small pool of blood.

'Lois?' he chokes. 'Don't…leave me.'

'Goodbye, Super-Duper-Man,' Mary wearily replies. 'You know what? That's the first time I've ever really seen you fly.'

Just as Mary is about to leave, a mouldy dishcloth catches her eye. She crosses the room and carefully stoops down to retrieve the crucifix that lies beneath it. It appears to be broken. Strange, she thinks, the pewter cross must have cracked when it landed. With a slight twist, Mary forces the two pieces apart. She throws the cross back into the corner and drops the dirty cloth back over it. Marvelling at the shiny little Jesus man in her hands, she notices something even stranger. He appears to be smiling, grinning from ear to ear. Planting a gentle kiss on his pewter head, she hitches up her dress and tucks him into her knickers. With a laborious stride, one hand on her pregnant belly and the other resting on Jesus, she shuffles out of the house and into the street.

Secret Santa

a.

Santa peers deep into the boy's glassy blue eyes, probing them for secrets. They are puffy red from crying and there is a faint yellow bruise beneath his left eye. All about them, the Moralpanik Mall is bustling with last-minute shoppers and ravenous seasonal consumers. Santa regards the boy's father, a short stump of a man with an air of restlessness and mean pride about him. He notes that his grip on his son's shoulder is iron-tight. The man pushes the boy towards Santa, urging him forward like a stubborn wooden chess piece. The boy's feet fight to keep pace with his body, staggering to another standstill. He doesn't want to move. He looks at the ground. Santa notices a wet stain on the crotch of his shorts.

'You go sit on Santa's lap and get your present, son,' the man says, attempting to sound cheerful and enthusiastic but instead appearing strained.

The boy still doesn't want to move. The man looks around them, his furtive eyes darting between the other Christmas shoppers and the families waiting in line behind them. Growing impatient, he shoves the boy again, this time more forcefully. The boy jerks forward and he falls to the ground.

'Shit,' the man hisses, moving to help him up. 'I'm sorry,' he says to everyone and no one in particular. 'He's so clumsy, he's…'

'I've got it,' Santa says calmly, cutting the man off and waving him away. He helps the boy to his feet and dusts him off. He affectionately ruffles his dark, curly hair.

The boy is uneasy on his feet but soon finds his balance.

Santa sits back on his tinsel throne and smiles gently at the boy. 'Ho-ho-ho! Now, what is your name?' he asks, thoughtfully stroking his beard.

The boy tentatively looks up, meeting Santa's eyes for the first time.

Before he can answer, the man interjects, 'Jim, his name is Jim!' he says. The words tumble from his mouth like spiders, final and emphatic, no negotiations.

'So, Jim, is it?' Santa asks.

The boy doesn't look comfortable.

'You are a very special boy, Jim. Do you know how I know that?'

The boy shakes his head.

'Well, I was looking over my Naughty and Nice lists the other day and you were at the very top. Do you know which list you were on, Jim?' Santa asks.

The boy shakes his head again, although now he is intrigued and his blue eyes widen in curiosity.

'You were at the very, very top of the Nice list, Jim!' Santa says.

The boy's mouth gapes open in wonder. His eyes fill with light. 'Did I win anything?' he asks hopefully, his shrill speaking voice now audible.

'Why yes, you did, Jim. You can have any present you like. What do you want from Santa this Christmas?'

The boy looks back at the man, who nods gravely, then back at Santa. He mumbles something incoherent and then looks back at the ground.

'What's that, Jim?' Santa asks, not hearing him. 'Here, you whisper in Santa's ear what you want,' he says. Santa leans forward and the boy obliges, speaking softly into his ear. Santa appears to be momentarily startled by the exchange.

Before he can reply, the man lunges at the boy, grabbing his arm and pulling him away. 'What did you say, boy?' he asks urgently.

'He told me what he wants for Christmas, Dad,' Santa says coolly.

'And what, pray tell, is that…Santa?' the man asks.

'Well, I can't say now can I…Dad? That would surely ruin the Christmas fun.'

'Let's go, boy,' the man snaps gruffly. 'Best get you home to your mother.'

'Wait!' Santa says. 'I have to give him his present.'

The man pauses, uncertain. Then, sensing he is making a scene, he momentarily releases the boy. The boy strides over to Santa, still shaken but with a renewed sense of purpose. Santa digs deep into the big red sack at his side, rummaging through the contents until he finds what he is looking for. He hands a brightly wrapped box to the boy and he eagerly grips it, but Santa doesn't let go of the package. He locks eyes with the boy and draws him to him, whispering confidentially into his ear. The boy nods like he understands and clasps the box tightly to his chest. It is deceptively heavy.

The man grabs the boy's shoulder, his grip tightening like a vice. He leads him away.

Santa scowls wryly as he watches them steadily fade from view. The scared little boy and his father, now gone, enveloped by all the other plastic Christmas families on display.

'Ho-ho-ho!' Santa chortles to the mother and daughter who are waiting next in line. 'Now, what's your name?' he asks the girl merrily.

The girl, lightning-in-a-blonde-bottle and used to getting her own way, marches straight up to Santa and confronts him. 'What did you say to him?' she demands.

Santa laughs heartily. It is obvious she has been watching the scene unfold intently and is more than a little curious.

'Tell me,' she says.

'Well, little miss, I told him that he can open his present whenever he wants to. Unlike you…' Santa playfully scolds, lightly tapping her button nose with his index finger, 'he doesn't have to wait.'

b.

Later that evening, Santa sits on a stool and rests his elbows on the main bar. His big red sack is on the floor beside him. Every now and then, he absently nudges it with his black boot, just to make certain it is still there. Its mysterious contents threaten to spill over and dot the tavern's stale, beer-drenched carpet with glitz and colourful detritus.

Santa half watches a television screen perched above the bar, streaming the major news stories of the day. 'Ho-ho-ho,' he drawls with slightly diminished Christmas cheer. 'Another double please, bartender!'

The bartender sidles over to him, all bazooka boobs, tight jeans and cynical grit. She pours him a drink and then stares at him quizzically. He's like a hard-boozing jigsaw puzzle, she thinks, an old-school charmer with reality issues and a genuine beard. He's still dressed for business, as per usual, although his red and white suit is saturated with ingrained sweat. The tendrils of his long white beard sweep the surface of the bar and mingle with peanut fragments and spilt booze. She's usually a natural at reading people, but there is something intangible about Santa, something that escapes her. Last week he showed her snapshots of what he called 'his kids' on a cheap mobile phone. They looked more like emaciated reindeer to her, posing like mangy pets in varying degrees of ill health. Still, she humoured him. 'Awwww… they're adorable,' she gushed in predictable tones, 'so cute.'

'Hey, turn that up!' Santa says suddenly, pointing with considerable emphasis at the television screen.

The bartender quickly complies with his request.

'An eight-year-old boy who was reported missing in February last year has been found,' the television says. 'In dramatic circumstances, young Jesse Talbot managed to escape from his captor, a yet unidentified man, by shooting him dead with a .38 pistol. According to police, the pair were driving across the south side of Moralpanik City when they stopped at traffic lights. The boy then used the gun on his kidnapper, firing it just once at point-blank range into the back of his head. It is unknown at this time when, where or how the boy acquired the weapon. He has been reunited with his family.'

Santa lifts his glass to the face on the screen and silently toasts the television. Then he throws back his head and downs his eleventh double whiskey in one huge festive gulp. A thunderous belch erupts deep from within his rotund belly and he farts wetly, licking his chapped lips.

The bartender rolls her eyes and pours Santa another drink.

'Merry Christmas, Jim,' Santa slurs dryly. 'Merry bloody Christmas.'

The Holy Babble

What would Jesus do?

That was the question Jesus asked himself when they first bailed him up and locked him away. The Messiah Ward was a brightly lit, antiseptic maze of cells, corridors and creeping psychiatric order. The asylum had other wards, each with their own individual purpose, but this one was deemed appropriate for Jesus. Apparently, he suffered from delusions of babblical grandeur. He was wrestled to the ground, bashed around the head and fitted with an ill-fitting straightjacket. Then they injected him in the temple with a glistening syringe of ink-black ooze. It was medication, they said. It would help him to get better, they said. It felt more like a prime-time sitcom lobotomy, all chaotic echo and canned laughter, throbbing behind his eyes and making his eardrums pound and itch.

He was the real Jesus, the true messiah, the son of God. Or was that simply what he had been led to believe? No, Jesus absolutely and irrevocably knew it to be the truth. The voice of God – his soothing companion, guide and friend – had been a constant presence in his mind, until now. Now God was being very quiet indeed. Was God afraid of the possibility of electroconvulsive therapy? Why was God in hiding? The silence was deafening. He felt eerily alone for the first time in a long time. It was a frightening sensation. It was as if his best friend had suddenly died and nobody else had noticed.

Apparently, Jesus's name was Fletcher Crumb now. It was on his laminated name tag, pinned to the breast of his strangulating straightjacket. If they were going to mock him, they at least could have slapped something more babblically appropriate there. No King of the

Jews, no INRI, just Fletcher damned Crumb. The moniker was oddly familiar to Jesus but he didn't know why. It didn't even remotely resonate with his sense of divine purpose.

Fletcher Crumb? No. Nope. No way.

What would Jesus do?

After forty days in solitary confinement, he was all but ready to concede. He was told by an ominous voice at regular intervals that if he rescinded his position, denied being the Messiah, the Christ, the One, et cetera, blah, blah, blah, they would let him out early. It was awfully tempting. They would feed him a hearty meal, they said, give him a cold beer and let him have a shower and a shave. All he needed to do was cop to just being an average guy with a limited grip on reality. Then they could get on with removing the cyber bug from the back of his neck. Jesus had assumed it was some sort of divine metallic pimple. As far back as he could remember, it had always been there. Yet when he attempted to think back far enough, his past seemed so blurred, so intangible. The last two years were vivid in his mind. But before that, it was almost as if he didn't exist. As for the so-called cyber bug, it was their property, they said. They wanted it back, they said. It had served its purpose and so had he, they said.

They said.

They said.

They said.

Christ! Jesus thought. This is ridiculous.

So, what would Jesus do?

When he was first released from solitary confinement, after serving the full forty days, Jesus was weary, weak and thin. So far, they had failed in their efforts to break him. He ate and bathed and gathered his strength but refused to shave off his beard. After a while, his mind began to clear and he slowly absorbed his new surroundings.

The Messiah Ward was relatively small and heavily fortified. Only the staff got in or out. There were no visitors allowed. Patients were regularly snuck up on and injected with ink black ooze; dragged away into back rooms where all sorts of unimagined horrors befell them. Unconscious or not, the dull echoes of their screams rang in Jesus's ears. Was it his overwhelming sense of empathy that allowed him such aural insights, Jesus wondered. Or was it simply in his overactive mind?

The staff members were a controlling, nasty lot. All the female nurses were covered in clown make-up and bore expressions of bored contempt. The male security staff were all burly muscle-bound types dressed in stylish pink tracksuits. The Pink Patrol carried electrically charged batons that resembled cattle prods and would use them multiple times on the same patient whenever they saw fit. They were not afraid to use excessive force if someone was even slightly disagreeable or difficult. The effect of the shocks caused instant, uncontrollable diarrhoea and often rendered the victim unconscious. The stench of shit and madness lingered in the air; bleach and burning flesh assaulted Jesus's nostrils. Everybody was afraid, yet Jesus could tell that they still clung to their versions of reality. But what were they exactly? A culture of fear, violence and intimidation was omnipresent. Everywhere Jesus looked, someone was being bullied into submission in the name of maintaining the appearance of sanity and order.

When Jesus counted the other patients, he realised there were exactly twelve of them. They were all male and had large laminated name tags bearing the titles of babblical apostles. Matthew, Mark, Luke and John were all there. There was a shifty-eyed, cynical Thomas, and even a Judas who appeared suitably friendly but probably possessed a shady demeanour of sly cunning. It was too soon to tell. Jesus decided he would try to make friends. He soon discovered, however, that none of them would answer to their names. They simply ignored him at first. Peter was particularly difficult.

After a series of rude snubs, Jesus leaned over and calmly whispered in his ear, 'But Peter, you are the rock on which I will build my church.'

Peter flew into a sanctimonious rage, swatting at Jesus as if he were a tenacious and particularly annoying mosquito. 'No, I'll build MY church on YOU if you don't leave me alone!' he screamed.

A few of the other patients echoed similar threats, raving competitively over the top of each other, things like 'YOU'RE the bloody rock, not ME. Piss off, you NUTTER!'

If they dared remove their name tags for any reason, the white-coat Pharisees and the Pink Patrol would threaten them with forty days in solitary or zap them repeatedly with powerful electric shocks. The thing that kept the lunatics in check was fear. 'God, they hated those name tags,' thought Jesus. Those rectangular laminated tags were the ultimate insult to their self-perceived sense of divinity and purpose. Twelve Messiahs, each one as convinced of their identity as the next. It was painful for Jesus to watch. The poor deluded souls, he thought. They hated the psychiatric staff and vice versa.

Every now and then, a nurse covered in clown make-up would burst into the smoking section of the asylum and sing out, 'Jesusss? Jeeesssuuusss?' as if she were calling for a family pet.

All heads in the area would promptly turn her way and chime in all at once, 'Yes?'

So, that's what Jesus would do.

'Fail!' the black-eyed nurse would exclaim and then laugh to herself. It was mean fun.

'You guysss are never getting out,' she would then hiss under her breath.

Jesus began to suspect that he was part of some twisted experiment. Why did his name tag have Fletcher Crumb emblazoned upon it? It was obviously a mistake. He didn't even get to be an apostle. What sort of cruel façade was this? The people needed him. His followers would be lost without him. Jesus had to get out of there.

Yet he realised that to gain release from the asylum he would have to play along to a certain degree. He agreed to have the divine pimple removed from the back of his neck. Jesus figured he didn't need it anyway and that seemed to be what they wanted from him most. He was told it would be an arduous process that would require that he surrender himself to a series of complicated surgeries. Without his consent, the process would be impossible, they said. The mysterious bug didn't want to let go of him. They told him that it would hurt a great deal and that afterwards he would not be the same. Jesus didn't believe them. He was certain that his divinity would protect him and that the process would do little to diminish his heavenly glow.

What Jesus didn't tell them was that, in the interim, he was determined to convert the twelve lunatics to his way of thinking. They needed to know that he loved them. He would forgive them for their sins, and if they wished to enter the pearly gates of his father's kingdom, they must accept him as their lord and saviour. It wasn't a complicated plan but it would test Jesus's capacity for communicating meaningful symbolic gestures and his knack for performing miracles. Admittedly, performing miracles had never been that much of a stretch for Jesus. They had always come easily and they tended to create a wow factor that could convert the most cynical unbeliever.

Outside the asylum, he had healed the sick and the lame. He made the blind to see. Those who were depressed he gave hope to and left them with a more chipper attitude than before. Even people who just happened to be a bit sad, in an irritable mood or plagued with a mild case of the sniffles, he cured. He relieved them of back pain, of headaches and, in the case of one deliriously tired lady, even insomnia. The latter had been a major coup; nobody saw that one coming. He could even turn water into wine and was subsequently immensely popular with alcoholics. Unfortunately, curing a hangover was the one trick that evaded him. Magically turning that self-same alcohol into his blood was a breeze. On the outside, they even had it tested. It was an exact match, same blood type and everything. So they bottled it and sold it to the devout public. But the average consumer tended to prefer it when it was wine, and as a result the blood did not sell well. The wine, however, sold like hot cakes.

They were not fake miracles. Surely, they were real. He had inspired everyone. He had been ridiculously, ludicrously popular and loved by everyone. Or so it had seemed to him at the time. Yet in the asylum,

Jesus knew that establishing himself would prove to be a monumental challenge. His timing and grace would need to be calculated to perfection to achieve his goal: absolute conversion. After which they would all be released together and with his new disciples by his side, Jesus could get on with spreading the good word.

Happy ending.

Team Jesus.

High fives all round.

In the asylum there would be no need for a crucifixion, thought Jesus. There would be no betrayals or denials, just good old-fashioned faith and lots of simplistic but inspirational sermons that everyone could understand. Oh, and perhaps a small display of symbolic martyrdom here and there, thus the apparently painful surgeries. Nothing radical, mind you. Jesus wasn't ready for the inevitable death and resurrection show. Not yet. He had too much work to do on the outside before things got too stressful. Jesus was self-aware. He knew he had a compulsion for helping people and a benevolent ego that, although requiring a certain degree of blind faith and subservience to remain buoyant, nevertheless needed to flourish and roam free to be beneficial to his troubled flock. The people needed a good shepherd and good shepherds can't protect and inspire humanity in an asylum, not on any grand scale.

One morning, as Jesus was sitting in the smoking section with some of the other patients, Peter appeared in the main corridor. There was a small sign sitting in the middle of the open area that led outside.

'CAUTION! SLIPPERY SURFACE!' it read.

The white tiles were glistening from shards of encroaching morning light. They had recently been mopped by the cleaner and were wet and soapy. Peter let out a loud dejected groan. All the others looked up at him and shook their heads. They dragged listlessly on their cigarettes and sipped cheap instant coffee. Peter muttered obscenities under his breath and lingered hopelessly on the other side of the ocean of shiny suds and bleach.

'What's he doing?' Jesus asked.

'He slept in,' said Simon wearily, idly flicking ash into a rusted tin can.

'Why isn't he coming outside for a smoke?' Jesus inquired curiously.

Peter looked very troubled indeed. He cocked his head to the side and pursed his lips, wondering whether to brave the dangerously slippery surface to have his first smoke of the day.

'You don't walk across the soapy water,' said Simon. 'Many have tried. It's just too dangerous. He'll have to wait, poor sod. The cleaner waits until it dries and then mops it again. There's a small window of opportunity in between but most of us just stay outside.'

Jesus finally saw his chance and knew he had to take it. It was one of those critical moments where inaction was not an option. He picked himself up and waited for the others to raise their heads. Then, he slowly paced towards the wet tiles.

'Don't do it, Fletcher,' one of them warned.

'It's not worth it,' another of them said, sensing Jesus was about to do something he would surely regret. 'You'll break a leg or crack your head open, dickhead. It's not safe.'

Gathering all his courage, Jesus nimbly began to traverse the tiled ocean. He made it look easy, graceful even. There was a gasp of wonderment from behind him as Jesus slowly and deliberately stepped over the sign and ever towards Peter on the other side. Peter looked shocked. He rubbed at his eyes, blinking in disbelief. A warm glow engulfed Jesus's head. His halo suddenly appeared above him. It had not been luminous since he first entered the asylum. Still, he continued to walk. Once in the very middle of the surrounding sea of tiled moisture, he stopped and held out his arms in a crucifix pose. He smiled kindly at Peter, who couldn't believe what he was seeing.

For Jesus walked upon the soapy water.

He did not slip nor did he drown.

Rapturous applause rang out from behind Jesus. The other apostles were cheering him on. Jesus motioned for Peter to join him. Peter shook his head again but then started to edge towards the lip of the wet surface. Jesus again beckoned him, but as soon as Peter's foot touched the outer tiles, he slipped and he fell. With a leap and then a dexterous slide, Jesus lunged towards him. Displaying amazing balance and finesse, Jesus broke Peter's fall before he could hit the water. Peter cried out in surprise; he looked up into Jesus's blue glowing eyes, framed by a heavenly halo, and began to weep tears of joy. Jesus grabbed Peter by the collar and began to drag him across the water to the other side, maintaining his own balance as he did so.

The other men whistled and cried out in unison, 'Hallelujah!'

For Jesus walked upon the soapy water.

He dragged Peter through the suds and sea on his wet arse unto the smoking section on the other side.

He did not slip nor did he drown.

Once upon the far concrete shore, Jesus yanked Peter to his feet and said to the other men, 'Someone give this man a durry.'

Two or three apostles raced to be the first to offer one of their precious smokes to Peter. But it was Jesus they stared at in wonderment. Jesus could see glee on their faces, but also confusion and bewildered awe. How had he done that? No one had ever braved the soapy water ocean and survived unscathed. Where did his magnificent halo come from? None of them had one. Why did he? It was about then that the disciple messiahs steadily began to question their own sense of identity. Who was this marvellous magician called Fletcher? Who were they in comparison? Were they mad? Were they insane? Was what they witnessed a miracle? Was it a shared hallucination? Why couldn't they perform miracles? But most important of all, they asked themselves, why wasn't he smoking?

When they asked him sometime later, Jesus said in a matter of fact tone, 'I just don't smoke.'

'But why?' they probed and prodded.

'For I am the Lamb of God, and as you know, sheep don't smoke,' Jesus said.

Still they badgered him. 'Why?'

'For I am the way and the light, you are the cigarettes and I am the Zippo. If you follow me, I will light you up,' Jesus waxed poetically.

'Sounds kinky,' said Mark with a grin.

'It isn't,' replied Jesus sternly, trying to keep matters serious and strictly babblical.

'So, we are cigarettes?' another of them asked.

'Yes, and I am the Zippo of Eternal Life,' Jesus continued, now on a roll.

'So, you don't need flints and fluid. You'll never stop lighting us up?' one of the men asked.

'Yes, for I am both the way to smoke and the Zippo that lights up the world.'

'So, the world is a cigarette too?'

'Yes, for I am the good shepherd and you are my flock,' Jesus countered, realising he needed to change tack. They were getting confused.

'Hang on. I thought you were a lamb? You can't be a shepherd and a sheep,' said Matthew.

'Yes, I am,' Jesus continued, enjoying the depth of the discussion but also growing weary of trying to come up with suitable metaphors, 'I am the non-smoking lamb and the shepherd who lights up the night with his eternal Zippo to ward off the wolves of the devil and protect his flock.'

'What about lung cancer?' Luke asked.

'What of it?' Jesus replied quizzically, not quite following.

Jesus was rather hoping they would latch onto the wolves and devil metaphor so he could run with it. He had spent a great deal of time thinking up sermons in solitary and had some juicy material saved up regarding desert werewolves and the temptations of the devil. But no, Luke wouldn't let go of the smoking thing.

'If a member of your flock gets lung cancer from smoking, will you cure them of it? I'm awfully worried about the dangers of smoking,' said Luke seriously, coughing self-consciously to illustrate his dilemma.

Yet before Jesus could intercede, Peter posed a rhetorical question. 'How can a cigarette get lung cancer? You're an idiot, Luke. We're durries. You heard him,' he said, looking to Jesus for confirmation that he was following his line of thought, even though he was secretly just as confused as the others. After the walking on water business and being rescued from the raging soapy sea, Peter was suddenly very keen to back up Jesus on every front. He felt an allegiance to the messianic Fletcher and was possessed of a new-found sense of loyalty. Jesus noted this sudden change in Peter and was well pleased.

'I think you're missing the point,' said Jesus knowingly, attempting to mask his delight at Peter's rather sudden conversion. 'In time, you will come to understand. Like sponges, you will absorb the majesty of my insights and follow the one true light.'

Thomas was getting very worked up by now. 'I'm not a sponge,' he said. 'I'll light my own cigarettes,' he said testily. 'For I am the true Messi–'

Jesus cut Thomas off mid-sentence. 'Enough!' he said.

Everyone went suddenly silent, waiting to see what the mysteriously Christlike Fletcher was about to do. Jesus glided over to Thomas and slowly waved his hands over the unlit cigarette dangling from the corner of his mouth. Miraculously, the tip burst into flame and then simmered into a smouldering bead of ash and smoke.

'Holy shit,' the apostle Mark gasped.

After that, everyone in the smoking section went eerily quiet. Suddenly it all made sense. It was a revelation.

For Jesus was the eternal light of the world.

He was a magical Zippo-sheep-shepherd who was far too aware of the dangers of smoking than to risk taking up the habit himself.

For Jesus was a holy enabler.

He was a lighter of cigarettes and the lunatics who smoked them.

Hallelujah!

Over time, and after many such sermons and illuminations, the twelve deluded Messiahs began to question their role in the scheme of things. They listened more and more to Jesus's wisdoms and began to see themselves as something other than divine. They were merely smoking sheep and they would follow Jesus's word to the letter. In turn, he would enlighten them and then hopefully, thought Luke, cure them of their impending emphysema.

Yet with every operation, Jesus grew more and more frail. His sermons became more obscure and his storytelling began to show signs of an inner decay. The surgeries were harsh and painful, and Jesus began to have memory lapses. He would awaken in some dim corner of the asylum and discover that three or four days had passed without his knowledge. His recollections were more like nightmares, snapshots of being tortured in dungeons with dirty, sweating walls. Strange, hairy-backed creatures licked incessantly at the back of his neck and humped his leg. Needles oozing dark drool were inserted in his spine and genitals like some form of poisonous, deep tissue acupuncture. His mind swam with images of literary vomit. He watched himself drowning in an ocean of phlegm from a distant shore. He felt warm, weeping alphabet-soup letters swim through his ears. They formed words he could not read and then dispersed, moving through his cranium and out the other side. He sat on an electric picnic blanket and drank chunky blood from a rusted can, as the bombs of Babble exploded all around him.

'Those devils, those greasepaint-smeared physicians of woe,' he thought. 'Damn their meddling evil ways.'

Jesus had something that they wanted and it seemed they would go to any lengths necessary to get at it. Somewhere in Jesus's muddled mind a realisation had taken hold: something very strange was inside of him, a creature of some kind, and it was refusing to let go.

When he was conscious, he dreamt of escaping the nightmare. His fantastical plans included flying through the ceiling with a wheelchair jet pack and leaving the asylum engulfed in flames. Search as he might though, he could not locate one. He also seriously considered burrowing down through the tiles under his bed with a spoon and getting lost in the web of tunnels he was certain were down there. The plan was just cunning enough that it might work. As long as no one looked under his bed, the staff would not suspect a thing until it was far too late. Although populated by giant chatty puffer fish, he believed the tunnels would eventually lead him to freedom. He stole a great deal of cutlery from the kitchen, spoons mainly. Yet he found the awkward angle required of him to remain under his bed for long hours, and the insistent scraping sounds of his tunnelling, eventually aroused too much suspicion.

Instead, Jesus took up smoking, hoping to blend in with the others and not be as much of an object of interest to the sadistic and arcane powers that throttled him almost daily. He constantly itched irritably at the lump on the back of his neck. He hoped it would decide to leave him and the torture would stop. He fainted several times, in full view of the disciples and staff, and again would wake up somewhere else. His head spun with nausea and the attacks continued unabated. When he felt himself drifting off into sleep or some form of ominous coma, he would kick and flail on his back like a dying insect. Jesus knew what followed; cornered again, he would thrash and froth and spit at the staff that descended upon him. When he awoke, another part of him was missing. He felt groggy and confused, wracked with a severe knife-like pain that seemed to wander all over his body, relocating every few minutes to manifest somewhere else and continue stabbing at his internal organs.

The disciples could only rouse Jesus's interest by calling him Fletcher or Fletch by then. He wouldn't answer to Jesus, to Christ or even to Zippo (as Thomas affectionately called him). It was distressing and heartbreaking for them to witness his gradual disintegration. His halo began to fade and flicker, almost as if their beloved Messiah was losing the will to glow.

'Who am I, really?' Jesus would ask himself. After a while, he found that he could no longer answer that question with any certainty. He was like a blow-up sex doll that when rattled or ravished would jangle with the evidence of a curious and complex inner creature. Something sentient that was protecting him from the puncture marks of the vampires that continually tried to find a way in. It was threaded throughout his emptiness, this creature without a name. It was as if the bones that kept him from falling apart, his muscle tissue and sinew and flesh had long since departed. They had been sucked out. Jesus was filled only with a moist, gaseous, pungent air. Yet the creature that fought to subsist in the void remained vigilant and resistant within him, fighting off every attack.

And it rattled when he shook, the creature, and it painted the inner walls of its flesh cage with ink black prayers… But for the first time it was afraid…for it was now alone…so it clung on for dear life… despite the death of its host, Jesus Christ…and the faltering will of a new, infinitely delirious landlord who went by the name of Fletcher Crumb.

The creature wasn't being asked to leave its home. It was being extracted, slowly, forced out blow by blow, brutally and painfully.

And so, the creature too began to doubt who or what it was. Demoted from divinity, it no longer saw itself as God. It could no longer peer out from behind the eyes of its host and marvel at all they imagined to be holy and real. There was nothing to create, nobody to inspire, no more magic in the box. It was alone.

So, without any further purpose or meaning to fulfil, the creature finally decided to let go. The most obvious route was chosen. The creature's grand exit was quite an ordeal for Fletcher. At the time, it felt as if a sacred temple known only to God had been torn asunder, ripped to pieces, obliterated, split right down the middle. The staff scooped the strange creature out of the rather unhappy toilet bowl and took it away. Fletcher could barely walk for days afterwards. When he did, he was not hard to locate. A winding trickle of gooey protoplasmic discharge followed him wherever he went. And much to the resident cleaner's emotional distress, wielding a mop and bucket, so did he. Wherever Jesus walked, the distraught cleaner followed closely behind.

On his final day inside the asylum, Fletcher Crumb brooded in the smoking section and stared blankly into the cracked concrete ground beneath his feet. The disciples kept their distance, casually casting nervous glances in his direction but not saying a word. They felt invisible. They felt betrayed. Their beloved Messiah was absent. In his place sat a hollow vessel, an empty coffin of a man with two deeply set eyes peering out of a wretched soul-casket. When the nurse called for Fletcher to gather up his things, Peter finally broke down. As Fletcher Crumb ambled clumsily towards the exit, he threw his head into his hands and wept like an abandoned child.

'He was going to build a church on top of me,' he sniffled, 'crazy bastard!' Peter continued to cry, only now he was laughing through the tears. 'God, I loved him, but it would have been the end of me for sure…'

Nobody said anything, but they all nodded at each other, silently agreeing it had been a close call for Peter. There had been a time when they believed their beloved Jesus could have done almost anything. It was reason enough to explain the distinct air of relief that had begun to mingle with their feelings of collective sorrow.

'Oh, Christ…' Thomas suddenly groaned in a deadpan manner. And looking warily up into the heavens as if something might suddenly fall from them at any moment, he said finally, 'He could have built a bloody church big enough to bury us all.'

A Public Disturbance

When Police Officer Nigel Tanner got the call that there was a public disturbance at the local Toys R Ploys store, it was close to the end of his shift. Considering he had been on his way across town to deal with an important family matter, it was particularly inconvenient. He figured he could radio-in from the car and explain to the sergeant that his pregnant daughter's waters had broken and, as his ex-wife was too fucked-up on drugs to drive, he was needed to take her to the hospital pronto. It would be a lie of course, but not an entirely implausible one.

After a few moments of deliberation, Tanner decided not to test his sergeant this time. His boss possessed an uncannily accurate bullshit-detector for a man of such an obviously vain disposition. That, and the fact that Tanner knew his daughter Mary wasn't going anywhere without money, left him with little recourse but to plough through the traffic towards the scene of the toy store disturbance.

His little girl of nineteen, ray of sunshine turned rebellious teen, Mary Tanner. She had apparently arrived at her former stepmother's house heavily pregnant, distraught and penniless with nowhere else to turn. Pam, Nigel's ex-wife and drug-addled zombie queen – he had been unhappily married to her for five twisted and excruciating years – once again couldn't deal with the situation. Nigel knew what Pam thought of her stepdaughter: nothing much at all. Unfortunately for Mary, who could be a tad naïve about people, she had never quite cottoned onto this fact. It was upsetting for Nigel because Pam was the first person his daughter went to when she was out in the cold. Mary was just too much of a trusting soul to figure out that her former stepmother didn't care about anyone but herself.

Mary's real mother died in a car accident when Mary was only four. Her heart had been broken before she was old enough to understand what a broken heart was. She just knew her mum had gone somewhere nice, like a place in the sky, and she wasn't coming back. Nigel hit the bottle hard and, for some inexplicable reason that still evaded him, he eventually married Pam, who was also an alcoholic. Mary was looked after by her grandmother during the whole sordid mess.

Nigel was amazed that Mary had survived at all, let alone turned out to be such a compassionate, if sometimes misguided and wilful young woman. Mary had the closest thing to a pure heart Nigel had ever encountered in a person. On the other hand, she was an absolute fool when it came to boyfriends. He hadn't met the latest specimen, but Nigel suspected he was a bit of a dick. Mary wouldn't let him meet the guy and that was always a bad sign.

Nigel Tanner figured he'd just stop off at the Toys R Ploys store on the way and deal with the offending individual as quickly as he could. He'd cut a few corners of course, maybe drag the guy out of the store and dump him at the Moralpanik Ministry Asylum. They'd know what to do with the loon: assess him, throw a straightjacket on him, then lock him up in solitary for a few months. After he'd calmed down, they'd link him up to one of those medication machines that were supposed to inspire sanity and a sense of competitive motivation in the mentally disturbed. What were they called again? Pokie Parlour Tranquillisers? Clunker Junk Pill Machines? He couldn't remember exactly, but it was something like that.

According to the police radio report the Toys R Ploys staff believed the guy in question was convinced he was a superhero, not to mention, he was naked and harassing customers with his free and easy heroic over-enthusiasm. A few zaps with the stun gun and he'd be a jelly doughnut, thought Tanner; easy to throw into the back of the squad car. He'd be a newly pacified delivery for the Moralpanik Ministry Asylum head shrinkers to process and then vegify. Yeah, he'd end up like all the other loonies, thought Tanner: dependent and despondent, addicted to a variety of mind-game blitz machines with impossible odds and no returns except for the shiny psycho pills that went right back in the damn machines anyway.

Tanner had an Uncle Clyde who went that way once. He was put away for urinating on the mayor in the middle of the Messiah Coronation Parade. It was funny as hell at the time. When they eventually let him out after a few years, processed and rehabilitated, he was dead behind the eyes. No life left in him that young Nigel Tanner could see anyway, and in some ways more of a junkie after that than a crazy. It was a sad but necessary process, reckoned Tanner. At least he wasn't a threat to anybody for a while – no more high-profile pranks or public indecency.

Then they say he broke back in to the asylum. It was almost unbelievable; no one could figure out how he did it. The place was rumoured to be like Fort Knox. When they found Uncle Clyde, he was in the hospital Gaming and Recreation Parlour draped over one of those mobile toilets with the squeaky mechanised legs, frothing from the mouth, unconscious and covered in gleaming gold pills. Seems Uncle Clyde got to one of the machines, cranked it up in the middle of the night when no one was around, and finally hit the jackpot. Nigel Tanner never did find out what the authorities or the asylum staff did with his uncle after that, but no one in the family ever heard from him again.

Tanner hadn't spoken to or seen his daughter Mary in a few months and had to admit that, despite his nothing-fazes-me demeanour, he'd been worried sick about her. She'd probably been dumped again by her on-again off-again jerk-off boyfriend – most likely the father of her child – and was in meltdown mode. He loved his daughter dearly but they had grown apart in recent years. When she insisted on keeping the baby, Nigel was not exactly pleased. His ex-wife Pam was too self-absorbed and stoned to give a shit.

So, Officer Tanner sped through the Palpitation Motorway traffic, police lights flashing unnecessarily, until he came to a screeching halt outside Toys R Ploys. He got out of the car and loosened his utility belt, just enough to allow him to grasp either the stun gun, his revolver or the truncheon, without his generous rolls of belly flab getting in the way of a clean and sudden draw.

'Take down this punk fast, Tanner,' he said to himself. 'Make it look easy.'

Joseph didn't see Officer Tanner approach him from behind. He was way too preoccupied with flying between the shelves and impressing the perplexed crowd. When the gentleman at the counter had refused to serve him, or to agree to exchange his faded little red cape for a full Super-Duper-Man costume, Joseph had morphed into full superhero mode. Although enraged and faux heroic all at once, his black eye and the dry blood caked around his mouth did little to prove to the onlooking parents and children that he was who he claimed to be: Super-Duper-Man. And his attempts at pirouetting and leaping large plastic Barbie mansions and Grey Skull castles in single super bounds had begun to tire him out. What would it take to persuade these petty mortals of his powers?

'Oh, sweet Mary,' he wept as he dipped and whirly-twirled like a deranged weasel between the aisles, 'It is I...your conqueror, your bleeding hero! Vanquished I was by your intangible womb and the cretin trapped therein. Oh, Mary...' he continued to warble pseudo poetically, 'I shall cometh home to thee and claim my rightful place in your enchanted clam!'

But then, just as Joseph uttered the words, 'Oh do letteth me back in...' he also felt the powerful crunch of Officer Nigel Tanner's truncheon connect with the back of his skull, snuffing out what little light there had been between his eyes and brain, in one sudden blow.

'Lights out... Dipshit!' crowed Tanner. The officer stood above Joseph's crumpled unconscious body and grinned in primitive triumph. 'Too easy!' he drawled.

As the thinning crowd of voyeuristic Toys R Ploys shoppers dispersed, Police Officer Nigel Tanner proudly adjusted his testicles.

Shifting them just a little to the left, he dragged the slain Super-Duper-Man out of the store to his waiting police car. Its lights brightly flashed a shade of neon blue, not unlike bruised Kryptonite.

If You Are Reading This, I Am Already Dead

In a crumbling, cockroach-infested unit block, hovering just a few stories above the mouth of the abyss, this story begins.

A thunderous clap of fictional urgency discovered Melvin Dilworth. At the time, he appeared to be a lost cause, rankled by an insufferable gloom and tagged by an army of confused shadows. An exceptionally unattractive man, Melvin was in his late thirties, had no close friends and was bound by an anxious, paranoid disposition. Melvin was sick of the world and it was sick of him. The babblical guilt and its literary manifestation, an omniscient god called Roger, had finally caught up with him. He was up against the brick wall of life, taking it none too subtly from almighty Roger, when a thought suddenly occurred to him:

Kill yourself.

After a pensive moment of reflection and a sip of black coffee, he decided suicide would be a good idea. In fact, it was the best idea he had ever had. Melvin slipped on his cracked reading glasses and a turtle-neck sweater mired by a shade of brown that mirrored his own life, armed himself with a cheap blue pen and began the process of drafting his suicide note.

I, Melvin Dilworth, am afflicted with a reality disorder. Although, I have no way of knowing whether those that led me to that conclusion are real or not. Perhaps they are just the pretty voices that I listen to when I'm lonely. Every now and then, I look back at the edge of the cliff that I just leapt from and wonder, was it worth jumping? I have concluded that it just might be, but I won't know for certain until I hit the ground.

I am a writer and I am writing to at least three of my other personalities; the other seven or so can piss off, or jump, whichever comes first. Those imbued with either true or heroic qualities (in a fictional sense) will meet me at the bottom of the cliff and we can compare the bloody splatter as ghosts, knowing what it means to truly hit rock bottom.

I am finished, waiting numbly for the test results and shaking, dancing in my head to the flatulent tones of a brass trumpet that was stolen by angels and never seen again. Yes, I am that far gone. Yes, I am the hero of my own musical tragedy. So, get used to the grinding of gears. Get ready for excuses. I can almost see the tears, the cascading romantic blubbering tears, gushing from the kind of river that floods your eyes and can unclog the most concrete of arteries.

I am perched on the quivering lip of a cavity so morose and rancid that not even Superman's deodorant could quell the stench of my failure. I'm teetering on the edge and wondering, was it worth it? I suppose it's no longer up to me...

The months went by slowly for Melvin. He wrote, at first, with great fervour. He whittled down his autobiographical ramblings from potential novel to short story to poem and finally, as the inspiration receded, to a disjointed pamphlet of his miseries. The well was drying up. Everything had the same tone. The same weary melody of loss played out in his head. Nothing was good enough. Soon he found he could no longer write at all. And so, on a nothing day in a nothing week with nothing worthwhile to write or say he attempted (again) to write down what would be his final words.

He pinned a blank page to the desk with his elbow and was surprised that it didn't struggle or attempt to get away. Instead it shifted in and out of focus, its unfriendly edges pooling on the wooden surface like milk. He fidgeted with the pen in his hands, scrutinising it under the bright light of his desk lamp, narrowing his eyes, glaring in such a way that a pen of suspicious character would surely admit everything and give itself up. The pen did not respond. He smirked. A vague feeling of satisfaction washed over him. The interrogation had been a success.

Melvin proceeded to drive the pen's nib into the soft skin of his temple. It had occurred to him that if he could get the tip close enough to where his thoughts gathered, they might somehow converge on paper. So far, he had been unsuccessful, and he had ugly marks on both sides of his head to prove it. He had tried inserting the writing device into his ear canal, but the wax had stopped the flow of ink. Besides, he thought, everyone knows that putting anything smaller than a fist inside your ear is dangerous, and Melvin certainly did not want to go deaf. He just wanted to end it all. The only thing holding him back was the note.

He wrote,

If you are reading this, I am already dead.

Was that it? Was that all he had to say? He had to leave something worthwhile behind; a lens through which others could view his tragic life and learn something from it. Melvin felt he needed to write something that would explain his absence from the world; a reason to be remembered. Perhaps I should look elsewhere, he thought, and write about something else for a change.

Melvin let his eyes linger over the blue pen in his hand. It seemed so charged with mystery, hollow and dark on the inside, yet filled with ink and unlimited potential. He placed it on the desk and watched it intently. Soon enough, the pen began to move of its own volition. The crude blue writing device rose, hovering above the page as if suspended by invisible wires.

It wrote,

Cedric trudged onward, the muscles in his legs strained under the weight of his armour. The tunnel had proved immense and seemed to have no intention of ending soon. But Cedric did not plan on returning the way he had come. The corpses of his comrades littered the entrance of the tunnel, and the echoes of their last moments of terror haunted him still. On the bright side, it was a stroke of fortune that he arrived late, or he might have died with them. They had agreed to rally together at dawn, but Cedric had overslept. Now he was the only one left alive, and he vowed he would succeed where so many others before him had failed. Hero, they would call him. He liked that, it had a nice ring to it. It was certainly better than being laughed at, spat on and ridiculed. Cedric tried not to dwell on why the people of his village treated him with such disdain. He had a job to do.

Melvin slid open his desk drawer, and the sight of its contents soothed him, alleviating his despair and frustration. With a delicate sigh, he perused his deadly arsenal: a handgun with four bullets, two bottles of prescription sleeping pills, a tattered paperback copy of *Jack Kevorkian – The Autobiography*, a dozen or so razor blades, and a lemon (Melvin was allergic to citrus fruit). It comforted him to see it all laid out so precisely. Just to know the pieces of the puzzle were there was enough. Melvin meticulously paced through the steps in his mind. He had given up trying to decide on one method and had formulated a plan that he believed was fool proof.

First, he would swallow all the sleeping pills. Then, as he waited for them to kick in, he would read the passages of Kevorkian's biography that he had underlined (the inspirational parts). When he felt the pills begin to take effect, he would slit his wrists with the razors, bite deeply into the lemon and, as the hives and swelling began to take hold, finally he would blow his brains out with the gun.

It was the perfect plan, flawlessly permanent and imaginatively fatal. Melvin was all but ready, except for one minor detail: the suicide note.

He let go of the pen in mid-air and it floated there, swaying to the soft ebb of his breathing, hypnotising him. Then it swooped upon the page, nib first, but gracefully, like a swan diving for pearls.

It wrote,

Cedric raised a burning torch above his head. A dark cylinder passed through the centre of the tunnel, meandering above him like the belly of a giant serpent. He briefly contemplated piercing it with his sword but decided against it. Swimming was not his strong suit. Rescuing beautiful maidens, however, certainly was.

Cedric once attempted to scale the battlements of a particularly ominous-looking tower, certain that a distressed maiden was trapped therein. He visited the tower every day for months, declaring in his most nonchalant and poetic tone that she let down her golden locks so that he might climb up and ravish her. With every pained silence, Cedric's resolve grew stronger, and his love more true. He developed complex theories to explain her reluctance to reply to his charms. Perhaps her hair was not yet long enough, and she was ashamed? Perhaps she was under the influence of a powerful magic spell that rendered her disinterested and shy? Maybe her evil captors had cut off her tongue, hacked off her limbs and chained her to the wall? Yet even if it were all true, if it so happened that she was indeed voiceless, limbless, and (heaven forbid) had short hair, Cedric vowed he would rescue, ravish and marry her nonetheless. And so, one fateful day, as the sun dissolved into the distant horizon and the haunting call of the curlew serenaded him, Cedric decided to climb the tower. With a grapple hook and length of rope he eventually managed to claw his way up to the elusive ledge. 'It is I, Cedric,' he cried in triumph. The old woman in the tower smashed him in the face with a frying pan. Cedric fell thirty feet to the ground.

He had avoided that tower ever since, certain that the maiden in question was simply not ready for a serious commitment, not to mention older than he had imagined. It was another part of Cedric's past that he would rather forget. So, he forged onward, flexing his pectorals as he did so, all the while whistling a tune he had heard somewhere before, but could not quite place.

Melvin sat back in his chair and attempted to gather his thoughts. He removed his spectacles and wiped the fog from the lenses. What was the point? He stood up and wandered into the kitchen to fix himself a coffee. Deformed cockroaches scattered the benches, scuttling over crumbs and swarming over his blurred vision. They fled as he waved them away, diseased soldiers, victims of recurrent blasts of cheap insecticide running from an unwinnable war.

Back at his desk, a steaming mug of sweet black coffee in tow, Melvin leant forward to peruse what he had just written. There was nothing there. No Cedric. No tunnel. No story. Melvin frantically rifled through the other pages. They were blank. He checked the floor and scanned the rest of the room. In a panic, he snatched up the pen. Gripping it with both hands and holding it aloft, he threatened to impale the blank page. Shaking in anger and disbelief, he carefully guided the nib of the pen onto the top left-hand corner of his canvas. The first words of his frustrated eulogy seemed to write themselves, his hand savagely carved a cryptic tattoo of characters onto the page. Pulling back from the desk and standing bolt upright, Melvin found himself gobsmacked by the view. He had written those same words, it seemed, hundreds of times before.

If you are reading this, I am already dead.

Exasperated, he slammed his pen down on the desk, screwed the paper up into a ball and flung it at the waste-paper basket in disgust. The paper sphere bounced off the rim and rolled across the carpet. It made absolutely no sense. Melvin threw his head into his hands and groaned for what felt like an eternity.

Soon, two solemn, ghostly strangers selling blue pens door to door entered Melvin's mind and proceeded to read his words. When they arrived at precisely this point of the story, they wrote this:

Cedric felt he could not continue further without at least a brief rest. He unsheathed his sword and sprawled against the dark curve of the tunnel wall, reflecting upon the strange stories that had spread the land.

According to popular consensus, a great omnipotent being, simply known as Melvin, had descended upon the Kingdom. A mysterious tunnel had appeared in the mountains. It was said to lead those who managed to brave its length into the sky, to a place high above the stratosphere, where the twinkling of stars was but a flickering memory of their death light years before. With the inexplicable appearance of the tunnel, the people of the surrounding lands had suddenly begun to disappear, as if wished out of existence by the twisted omniscience of a mad scribe. They were drawn to the tunnel in their hundreds: wannabe heroes and heroines, downtrodden slaves and noblemen, disgruntled housewives and crackpot hippies, all of them driven by the promise of a place in the sky. They died in their hundreds too, devoured by the incalculable length of the passage and crudely regurgitated, vomited from its vile mouth. The strange part, though, the bit that had really begun to scare people, was that every single one of them was lathered in a mysterious blue toxin.

After a few months, people had begun to speculate that the whole bit about a paradise in the sky was just spiritual propaganda. This didn't concern Cedric. He didn't really want to live in the sky anyway. The tower incident had left him with a crippling fear of heights, not to mention an irrational suspicion of pots and pans. But he was smitten with certain parts of the legend all the same, particularly the part that spoke of a mighty warrior who would come and save everyone: The Chosen Guy.

This was where Cedric figured he came into the equation. He would conquer the tunnel, face the one they called Melvin, and free his people. He wasn't too sure about the exact details of it all though. Like, whether this Melvin fellow was bigger than he was, it could be a problem if he was. And precisely how did all this tunnel travel free his people? He did not even know most of them. The one thing that Cedric was certain of, however, was that he would be showered with praise and adulation. And most importantly, the people of his village would stop laughing at him.

Melvin cupped his face in his hands and rocked back and forth in despair. What a waste. He was no closer to death than he was four months ago. He glared at the pen in disgust, lying there on his desk, looking smug and self-assured. There was no point blaming the paper, if he was going to accuse anyone it would have to be the pen. It truly deserved his wrath. Melvin snatched it up and held it to the light. 'You. Cannot. Be. Trusted,' he hissed. 'Yeah, that means you, mister,' he said, angrily waving the pen through the air above his head. Without a second thought, Melvin viciously snapped the pen in two. Blue ink splattered across his face and chest like buckshot, raining down upon his vengeful smile.

If the pen were still able to write, it would have written this:

Cedric lurched suddenly backwards as an explosion of light engulfed the tunnel up ahead. He would have thought many things in those final moments; about his estranged family; about true love and maidens trapped in towers with ridiculously long hair; about the powerful sorcery that was to steal his destiny from him; that if only he had reached for his sword in time. But Cedric did not get time to think at all. In fact, the last thing he heard wasn't the ferocious swell of a dark blue tidal wave. Nor was it the cracking of his own bones as he was dragged forever under. No, for Cedric it was more terrible than that. His ears rang with the echoes of a cruel and pointed laughter; the mad cackle of derision that had haunted him all his life. Yet somehow, Cedric knew that he was being taunted for the last time.

Melvin marvelled at his handiwork, the scattered guts of the pen sprawled out before him, dark ink trickling down his arms in noxious rivulets of shame. It was an all too familiar scene. Pen after pen had betrayed him and met the same tragic end. Yet this time it seemed different somehow, but he couldn't think why. Because just for a moment, for a brief fleeting second, Melvin regretted what he had done. Instead of reaching for another pen, his eyes welled with tears. Something deep inside Melvin Dilworth had broken in two.

After a few more moments of confused sobbing, Melvin noticed a neatly stacked ream of papers sitting under the waste-paper basket. How strange, he thought. It had not been there a moment ago. Ever so tenuously, he picked the pages up, nervously scanning the room for signs of intrusion or interference. It was a short story, scrawled in blue ink. Melvin recognised his own handwriting immediately. A sense of curious calm washed over him. He lowered himself onto the ink-stained floor and just lay there for a while, with the story clasped firmly in his hands. Death will have to wait, he thought; the suicide postponed indefinitely, at least until he could figure out a more literary reason to end it all.

Lashings of ink dried upon his skin and congealed in his thinning hair, bathing him in the dark blue blood of yet another murdered pen. Homing in on the first page of the story in his hands, Melvin was immediately struck by the familiarity of the words before him:

In a crumbling, cockroach-infested unit block, hovering just a few stories above the mouth of the abyss, this story begins.

Stranger

Late at night, as the dogs bark at shadows and the ticking of the wall clock slows to a heartbeat, Fletcher Crumb sits quietly in the darkness. Cockroaches worship his naked feet, scuttling to the rhythm of his breath. He ignores their lustful groans, choosing instead to marvel at the absence of shapes in his bedroom, as infinite as a world without eyes. The windows are plastered with layers of newspaper and wood glue, to murder the probing eyes of the street lamp. If God created the universe in seven days, Fletcher destroys it in the small hours, with the simple flick of a light switch.

There is a loud knock at the door. It is a sound he has been expecting for some days. Yet instead of bounding to his feet and answering it, Fletcher Crumb merely sits still in the darkness, waiting. When he is satisfied the knocker has gone, leaving the object he ordered by the door, he rises to his feet and creeps outside. Careful to shield his eyes from the stairway light, he snatches up the package and carries it inside. It is rectangular and flat, two feet by five, wrapped in crisp brown paper and bound with string. Fletcher is relieved and thankful. He strokes the telephone like a favourite pet, pleased with its obedience; home delivered and no need for any agonising small talk.

He hoists the package above his head and edges slowly across the darkened room, blindly navigating a path through the remains of his ruined furniture. When he reaches the far end of the flat, he leans the object against the wall. His eyes adjust themselves slowly and patches of purple and green radiance smother his vision. Then, it is absolutely and utterly dark. There is nothing for Fletcher to see but the pattern of light that is trapped in his eyes. To turn on the light would be foolish, he thinks. There will be time for that later. He caresses the mysterious package, running his fingers slowly across its edges, he breathes in the scent of the fresh paper. It fills him with a strange sense of danger, a mingling of fear and excitement. He thrills at his own courage: to purchase the enemy; to invite it into his own home.

He stands up and steers his way into the kitchen, dragging his hand across the wall until he finds the doorway. He grasps the cold steel handle of the refrigerator and opens it eagerly. Fletcher has removed the automatic light, and rummages through the shelves, fumbling for a moment before he finds what he is searching for: a small ceramic bowl of top-grade heart-smart mince, raw and untainted by flame. It is a guilty pleasure, but one that keeps him strong and sharp. The salty, rich texture, combined with a low-fat content to rival the leanest steak, is simply delicious. But compared to blades of fresh beef, Fletcher finds that mince generally lacks the free-flowing juices, the blood. Most steak, like rump and fillets, though exquisite, Fletcher finds to be a tough meal. He possesses unusually sharp teeth, but it is still difficult, an exercise in gnawing, noisy slurping and chewing. And even then, the remainder of the slab, like a drained corpse, is simply too hard to swallow. Fletcher throws it away. Heart-smart mince, which he purchases from the local butcher shop, is reasonably priced and easily digested. It is perfect for a tasty late-night snack and food for endless thought.

Fletcher is concerned that his diet, consisting entirely of raw meat, could possibly be construed as unconventional. It makes him feel guilty, thinking of all the magnificent animals that have died horrible deaths to fill his belly. Although, he feels just as sorry for cumquats and salad onions; they have been neglected, he thinks, and deeply misunderstood. When a person cries while cutting up an onion, it is a sign, surely. 'Feel my pain,' the onion is saying. 'You're hurting me.' It has nothing to do with science. As far as Fletcher Crumb is concerned, broccoli could conceivably possess a soul too. It is possible that it has feelings and feels pain.

Fletcher Crumb sits on the edge of his bed, picking at the bowl of raw mince in the darkness of his unit. He considers his predicament for the millionth time.

The Impostor is everywhere. He wants to do bad things to people, terrible things. Fletcher is going to catch him out. He is going to kill him. The only question is how?

Fletcher needs his eyes to see the darkness that soothes him. Without eyes to see the darkness, it is no longer real. To recognise something that is not there, to know the absence of reflection, Fletcher Crumb needs his sight. When he closes his eyes, which he sometimes does to avoid a mirror or a pane of glass, he knows that the Impostor is still there, outside, waiting, urging him to open his eyes and smash it to pieces.

Fletcher momentarily considers that it might have something to do with an unknown part of his own psyche; a vision of perverted reality, a subconscious inferno unaware of its own rising heat. Perhaps the warping of his own image is a mental projection of his inverted loveliness? No. That is ridiculous, unthinkable. He scoffs down the last remnants of mince and marvels as a figure suddenly appears, suspended as if by angels in the darkness above his eyes. He recognises himself immediately, and the splendour is indescribable. His grace is miraculous. He watches, transfixed, as the image slowly fades, consumed by a creeping fog. The last raw particles of mince slowly dissolve on his tongue until he is once again alone.

Was it an illusion? That was the real me, he thinks, not the Impostor. But Fletcher Crumb still has his doubts. Can he really trust his eyes? After all, isn't it merely another mirage, a cheap magic trick caught in his easily deceived eye? Whatever it was, and wherever it came from, there was no denying it was out there, external, apart from him.

The Impostor is up to mischief.

He is a dangerous and cunning foe.

He must be stopped at all costs.

Because Fletcher is terrified of the Impostor, he does everything he can to avoid him. He hides from anything that might aid reflections of any kind, particularly light. Mirrors fill him with boundless dread, raping the mental portrait that he cherishes and replacing it with a cruel lie. He has little idea how they do it, but every mirror he investigates warps his undeniably handsome face, making it appear hideous and repulsive. Certain bodies of water are almost as bad. A flood he feels he can handle, but murky ponds and dark, perfumed toilet water frighten him. Fletcher knows it is not himself staring back from the septic depths. No, it is the Impostor. The water's mercurial eye molests his features, making him seem ugly and deformed.

Fletcher Crumb has lived in Moralpanik for as long as he can remember and for as long as he cannot. He is a nervous dreamer and a vindictive optimist. After being released from the Moralpanik Ministry Asylum, Fletcher was placed here by the government housing agency Centre-Slink; left to his own dubious devices in an unremarkable yet tastefully modern one-bedroom unit. Fletcher is the official tenant of Unit 12, in a block of thirty identical yet tastefully modern units. Although, to say that he has not upheld Centre-Slink's strict code of cleanliness, maintenance and order would be a laughable understatement. He lives in filth and squalor and will possibly be forcibly removed from his abode pending the next Centre-Slink inspection. Fletcher doesn't much care about their three strikes and you're out policy. There are more important things for him to worry about. He does, however, feel fortunate to live on the second floor, as it means he can avoid the tyranny of random flooding.

Fletcher yearns for destruction, for floods, storms and cyclones to descend upon the city. Moralpanik has a reputation for extremities, but unfortunately for Fletcher, they rarely manifest in the form of natural disasters. There's nothing remotely natural about Moralpanik's real calamities. Fair weather brings the worst out in people, Fletcher thinks, and a flood is just what the city needs. So, he fantasises about storms, about a flood of babblical proportions. He is Noah, except the cool loner version, without all the animals and the wife and the big boat. He imagines soaring above the crest of a mighty wave in his little unit.

At the very least, an unexpected flood would most surely drown the young couple living in the unit directly below him (or at least ruin their furniture). Fletcher Crumb has not met Tiffany and George Best yet, but he already hates them, intensely. They fight and bicker constantly and as a result they often appear as characters in his dreams. When they do, Fletcher tries to kill them. It is his own special form of dream management, and if anybody in his dream hasn't been formally invited, they must die. But almost every time he sleeps and dreams, his attempts at inter-dream slaughter also fail, miserably and irrevocably. And like a sloppily conceived double homicide, the ramifications are endless. He wakes up feeling powerless, over and over again.

Tiffany and George are either oblivious to the racket they make, or they don't care. They are as indifferent to their loud moans and groans of pleasure as they are to broadcasts of their hatred for one other. The effect of their frequent bouts of deafening affection has been horrifying. Fletcher feels that they have caused him irreparable psychological damage and they must pay. The last thing he wants is a vivid mental picture of Tiffany whipping George's pasty white buttocks with an eggbeater. But that's what he gets, night after night.

Although it is always threatening to rain in Moralpanik, in truth, it rarely does. In fact, it has been so long since Fletcher has seen rain, since he has felt it course down his cheeks like tears, that he sometimes doubts that it has ever rained at all. Perhaps he imagined it. Perhaps, like so many things Fletcher thinks is beautiful, it only exists as an idea, a symbol. The fact that it might not be real makes it even more beautiful…and dangerous too. His memories of rain, like everything else, no longer feel like his own.

Fletcher is like the storm, the violent flood; he is beautiful because he destroys things. He dismantles, dismembers and destroys anything he can get his hands on; in the dark too, which is quite a trick. The television is in pieces. He took to the toaster with a baseball bat and picked holes in the mattress when he was bored, like a crow, pecking the eyes from a desert carcass. His furniture is in ruins but he can no longer see it, so the devastation is cloaked in darkness. Once he even put the microwave in to get fixed after an unfortunate accident with a bowling ball on ten-minute defrost, just so he could do it all over again. The refrigerator pissed gas for three days when he stabbed the freezer wall with a knife, and he still has dizzy spells from the fallout. The only thing that escaped his wrath was the telephone. Fletcher likes to dial random numbers and scream into the receiver when an unlucky victim answers the call, and boy do they crap themselves.

If Fletcher cannot control something, he wants to get rid of it, smash it, or at least pretend it isn't there for as long as he can. The results are often disastrous, and the difference between reality and fantasy has become harder and harder for him to discern. Perhaps there has never really been a difference. It is all part of the same nightmare. Whether he is asleep or awake, it adds up to the same thing. He attempts to commit terrible atrocities in the name of dream management, and when he awakens, he pays for those crimes with his conscience and then he dreams and yearns to kill some more. He murders the light. He murders logic and love and desire, anything that might interfere with the utopian vision of his own true self: The Fletcher Crumb that Moralpanik refuses to acknowledge, reflect or understand.

The Impostor, as Fletcher knows him, does not look, sound, smell, feel or even taste like Fletcher at all. But the fucker is there every time he looks in a mirror: a pale ghostly streak of shit with cunning eyes and crooked teeth, grinning like a loon and smelling like death. When Fletcher speaks, his voice sounds alien and unfamiliar. It is as if a stranger is echoing the words that form in his head. And sometimes they aren't his words at all.

One night he awoke from a particularly murderous slumber. In his dream he was strangling George, his neighbour, with a length of electrical cord. George was berating Tiffany for being lazy. George's face was blue from the cord, but he seemed more concerned with his wife than Fletcher's ongoing attempt to kill him. He effortlessly wriggled out of Fletcher's grip and Tiffany began to complain, mid-dream, about a nauseating stench. It was not the failed murder attempt that woke Fletcher from his dream. He was accustomed to nightmares involving his neighbours ending that way. Rather it was what Tiffany said. 'You stink you stink you stink,' she wailed. Fletcher could smell it too, in the middle of his dream, which was strange, because he had never been aware of smells while he slept. He leapt out of bed and inhaled deeply, immediately realising something did not smell right. The aroma was alien and unfamiliar. When he inhaled, a disgusting combination of castor oil, sour cream and rotten fish filled his nostrils. He scoured the darkened flat for the origin of the scent. He tore apart pillows and ripped at the stained carpet. He discovered nothing. Until eventually, after much deliberation, he considered the unthinkable, that the scent emanated from himself.

But it was not his smell. No. It simply couldn't be. He hadn't bathed for months, but this smell was different, it was utterly foul and repugnant. He finally decided that the scent must be that of the Impostor, stealing the last semblance of his identity and overwhelming his own body odour with its vile stench.

Certain senses are easier to cope with than his vision. He rarely speaks, even to himself, and he finds that if he ritually camouflages the overwhelming stench with copious amounts of cheap deodorant, it nullifies the problem. Sure, he doesn't smell like himself, and he doesn't sound like it either. But he can hide the problem, or alter it, for a little while at least.

It doesn't end there. When he reads a book by candlelight, he recognises the Impostor in the words. It is everywhere. Even shadows, which he sees as creeping distortions of the Impostor, make his pulse quicken and his palms sweat. They stalk him wherever he goes, attaching themselves to his ankles and refusing to let go.

Fletcher suspects that the heart that beats within his chest is no longer his own.

*

When Fletcher was first released from the Moralpanik Ministry Asylum, his regular doctor referred him to a psychiatrist. Fletcher was dubious. He was certain that he was not insane. Fletcher had genuine problems, but he doubted that medication or psychotherapy would help. He went along anyway. Fletcher remembers it all quite clearly, unfolding in his mind's eye in the safety of the surrounding darkness.

Doctor Crest wears an old blue suit, with flared pants and tarnished silver cufflinks. His face is crude and sallow and a constant chain of cigarettes dangle from the corner of his mouth. If he isn't lighting one up, he is stubbing one out. He rarely inhales, visibly at least. The smoke just seems to waft up into his nostrils as if it knows where to go. His laugh is low and sickly, and it litters his speech patterns, popping up at the most unpredictable moments. Fletcher isn't sure if his sense of mirth is cruel or simply compulsive. His nose is tilted to one side of his face and angry red. His eyes are like raisins, small and dark, and Fletcher feels uncertain exactly where he is looking in the room, because his pupils are swallowed up by shadow. But he seems keen to help, if abrupt, and Fletcher duly notes that there are lots of fancy letters after his name.

The doctor slurs one minute and is clear and incisive the next. He has a hip flask of vodka stashed in the bottom draw of his desk, and he often retrieves it as Fletcher speaks. He swivels his chair so that he is facing away, uncaps and then swallows. He assumes that his patients don't suspect a thing and considers most of them uneducated and naïve. He delights in dazzling his patients with his rich vocabulary. He likes nothing more than to see confusion on a patient's face – or, better still, feigned comprehension, where a patient is so startled by the calibre of the doctor's intelligence that they just nod the whole time, pretending they understand.

Fletcher wants immediate action, for tests to be carried out. He demands the assistance of research teams, of professors of reality, and paranormal psychologists. He stresses over and over, with little explanation or elaboration, that the problem is not in his mind. It is inherent in the universe that reflects him.

Fletcher refuses to talk of his family or childhood, believing it has no relevance to the creeping distortions that haunt him. The nature of his dilemma is arcane, he says, not psychotic. For the first few visits Fletcher deflects Doctor Crest's questions with questions of his own.

When the doctor skirts the issue and diverts the attention back onto his patient, Fletcher insists that his own past does not exist. 'How can I talk about a childhood that I have never experienced?' he says.

Crest laughs so hard he almost goes blue, and he only recovers by swivelling, uncapping, and taking another hit of vodka. 'How did you come into the world then, Fletcher? Who named you? Who changed your dirty nappies?' the doctor cajoles, teasing his patient to respond.

Fletcher insists he has no knowledge of such a past. It isn't that he cannot remember, he says, but that it simply never took place. 'It's the world that needs its nappies changed,' he says, 'not me.'

Fletcher is adamant that he did not enter the world in the usual way.

Doctor Crest is persistent but aggressive, certain that Fletcher has buried the details of some terrible past abuse. Parts of the puzzle are missing and Fletcher refuses to reveal them.

'If the Good Doctor,' Fletcher says, waving a finger in the doctor's direction, 'will reveal in detail the nature of his own neurosis and the childhood experiences that preceded it, then perhaps his patient will comply.'

'Fletcher,' Crest sternly replies, 'I am the doctor and you are my patient. I am bound by the nature of my profession to do no such thing.'

Swivel. Uncap. Swallow.

The doctor is unaccustomed to such resilience, let alone prying.

Fletcher jumps to his feet, knocking over his chair. 'My predicament is real,' he announces, 'and I am in grave danger of…of…'

'Misrepresentation?' the doctor quips, and a smarmy expression settles on his face.

Fletcher sits down. He locks eyes with the doctor., 'Very well,' he snarls. 'If, as your patient, I am bound to talk of a childhood that does not exist, I will do just that.'

And so, the floodgates open…

In the following weeks Fletcher recounts numerous stories from a past that he insists does not exist. His telling swerves from fairy tale bliss to torment and devastation. Fletcher talks of a boy's imaginary tormentor, a powerful giant who punishes him for his moral transgressions. Lashing and beating the boy with his giant hands, and always bringing him back to the mirror, to see the maggot that exists therein. The maggot that reminds the boy who he is and all he will ever be.

The boy feels that the giant can see inside his mind, teaching him that his thoughts are actions and that his hideous dreams are a mirror to his soul. Fletcher recounts it all, the memories of a past that does not exist, an imaginary history ruled by fear and fantasy. Fletcher sees it all, the maggot and the imaginary tormentor, through the eyes of a little boy.

The giant, with his rubbery pockmarked face and his piercing stare, glares into the boy's eyes, searching for a reason to punish the boy, looking for signs of guilt. The boy doesn't know what he's done wrong, but he feels guilty. He always feels guilty when the giant has been drinking. When he looks at the boy like the giant knows something the boy does not. He is guilty, and the giant can tell. The giant's breath is hot and stinks of the drink, and the boy turns his face away. The giant grabs the boy by the hair and drags him into the bathroom, standing him in front of the mirror. The boy doesn't so much as whimper, he looks at the floor, anywhere but in the mirror. He wants to be anywhere but here. He thinks about running away and the guilt washes over him like the giant's hot stinky breath.

Whack!

The giant delivers a blow to the back of the Boy's head.

Whack!

The giant pulls his hair back and forces the boy to look at the mirror.

The giant doesn't have to ask any more, the boy knows what is expected of him.

'Maggot,' he says, pointing at the smaller of the two figures in the glass. The giant nods and ruffles the boy's hair, almost affectionately. The giant is suddenly pleased with the boy. The giant grunts and staggers out of the bathroom.

The boy feels he has been good, and he stands like that, staring at the maggot in the mirror, the little maggot with tears streaming down his cheeks.

'Is this imaginary giant your father? Is he God? Are you really the little boy in these stories?' Doctor Crest asks.

'No,' Fletcher replies irritably, 'as I explained to you at our first meeting, this is an imaginary childhood. I have no such past. These are memories and dreams, certainly, but they are not mine.'

'Who is this boy that you talk of then? Surely you are not making all of this up?'

'Oh no,' Fletcher replies. 'He's just someone I knew once, a long time ago.'

'When you say knew, what exactly do you mean?'

'He's dead,' Fletcher replies uncomfortably.

'How did he die, Fletcher?'

'He was…murdered.' Fletcher feels suddenly sad, and he traces his finger across the desk, writing invisible words into the wood. When he speaks, his voice is distant and hollow, clouded by reminiscence and loss. 'I used to see him in mirrors, panes of glass, that sort of thing. I talked to him a lot, but I wouldn't say that we were friends. I came to know him quite well though. I almost felt like I could see through his eyes, like we were connected or something. It was strange, but he's gone now. He's been replaced, replaced by something monstrous, something too terrible to comprehend…'

Fletcher's voice trails off and his eyes mist over. He tilts his head to the side, as if he is listening to a voice that only he can hear. He grips his chair, searching the walls and ceiling for a crack or an exit, for a place to rest his eyes. There is a long silence, a dreamlike pause. The doctor stubs out a cigarette and the tiny fizzle of ash and fire echo in Fletcher's ears. The doctor doesn't ask Fletcher who murdered the boy, maybe he already knows.

Maybe.

'This tells me a lot about you, Fletcher,' he says, breaking the mood. His authoritarian tone, although professional and crisp, cannot hide the effects of the alcohol. 'Sometimes the truth is revealed in what one does not say, in what one infers. I think it would help if I put you on a course of medication.'

Suddenly, the doctor's head slumps onto the desk and he begins to snore loudly. Fletcher reaches over and shakes his shoulders vigorously to wake him. The doctor jumps up as if startled.

'You have a reality disorder, Fletcher, and these pills will help,' he drawls.

'My predicament is real,' Fletcher cries indignantly, 'and I am in grave and immediate danger of…of…' He stammers and looks wildly about the room for a word or picture that might inspire his outrage.

'Of what, Fletcher?' the doctor slurs, urging a premature response.

'Of…of…it,' Fletcher says, and his eyes again well with tears.

The doctor smiles sympathetically, to reassure his patient, and then burps loudly, ruining the moment.

'I can't control him, doctor, I just can't,' Fletcher weeps.

'I'll see you next week, Fletcher. We have much to talk about,' the doctor says, signalling that the session is at an end. He reaches into a draw and hands Fletcher a bottle of pills, retrieving his hip flask at the same time. The doctor uncaps and swallows, in front of Fletcher, and then mutters, 'Take two of these before bed and two in the morning.'

Fletcher takes the bottle and rattles it next to his ear. He doesn't care much for the label. Reality disorder? It makes it sound like he has a thought disease. But if they knock him out at night, it is worth it. As he leaves the room, he hears the doctor's head connect with the table again. So he goes back and carefully peels the doctor's fingers from his precious hip flask and takes it with him.

When Fletcher reaches home, he washes down the entire bottle of small pink pills with the vodka.

Blackout.

When Fletcher wakes up, he is face down in a puddle of his own dribble. He senses changes, loss of time, hours hidden, days missing. The wall clock is ticking erratically, now out of step with his pulse. The universe is rapidly contracting, and his awareness of its new size and his comparative sense of self, expands at a frightening pace. He grows in stature as the walls close in. The darkness implodes and still he grows, towering above the emptiness. So immense does he grow, so self-important, that he feels he may very well suffocate in the jaws of the vacuum.

The giant sits the boy in front of the mirror and cuts his hair. The boy sits as still as he can, and the giant squints his eyes, red with the drink, and hacks off big chunks of the boy's hair. The boy left the scissors at school, so to teach him a lesson the giant cuts his hair with an old-fashioned shaving razor. The boy wets himself, and hot piss trickles down his legs and onto the hair on the floor. The giant's face twists into disgust, and he cannot look at the boy. Before he leaves, he tells the boy to clean himself up and go to bed. The boy knows it is the maggot's fault, not his. He sits there glaring at the maggot in the mirror, just like the giant glares at him. 'You disgust me,' he says.

The next morning the giant sends the boy to school.

The boy sits staring at the teacher standing in front of the blackboard. He is aware of the other boys seated behind him, whispering and giggling whenever the teacher turns away. The boy knows they are making fun of him. Little missiles of warm spittle and paper sting the back of his neck. One slides under his collar and he can feel it slowly trickle down his spine. One side of his scalp is clipped short and the other is long and uncut. The teacher turns away, and the missiles hiss past his ears and stick in what is left of his hair. After class he deliberately pisses himself again. He hopes that if he stinks of piss, they will leave him alone.

*

Fletcher leaps up and grabs the package. He holds it to himself, promising it, whispering to it that he will open it, set it free. He will finally turn on the light and face the image trapped therein. He'd like to demolish it with the remains of the vacuum cleaner, nothing would be sweeter. But if he is right about his latest purchase, and he has a strong feeling he might be, he'll have no reason for destruction.

Why?

Because of the brochure he found in the street.

Because of the brochure he feels certain found him.

Fletcher picked it up off the footpath on his way to the Moralpanik Mall. It blew across the road, swirling on ghostly air currents, and landed at his feet. He thought it odd at the time because it was a still and windless day. It must be a sign then, he thought, the significance of which he would carefully consider. The slogan on the front cover was almost too good to be true. It was a promise, a spiritual revelation:

ABSOLUTE CLARITY OR YOUR MONEY BACK!
GUARANTEED!

The words offered Fletcher Crumb something he had been searching for, in a mirror, for a very long time.

Hope

'The Lucidity Le Grande' is a classic, the Mirror of Mirrors,' the brochure said. 'It comes with a gold-plated frame and guaranteed flush surface. No unnecessary distortion and no warping or misrepresentation.'

According to the small type, it was designed to overlook sudden and unfair weight gain and the temporary effects of a virus or foul mood. Skin blotching, random outbreaks of acne and other transient imperfections, the mirror would ignore. Anything that might mar the owner's flawless complexion, the mirror would pardon. For three, monthly credit card instalments of fifty-nine ninety-five, plus four dollars ninety-five postage and handling, you got the mirror, and for a limited time a free one-year subscription to the Vanity Fear Consumer Catalogue. With an impossibly detailed resolution and a no-questions-asked, twelve-month money-back warranty, Fletcher couldn't lose. Finally, the Real Fletcher Crumb – Guaranteed!

*

Fletcher paces the floor of his unit in imperfect circles. After each revolution, he returns to the package to run his hand over the crisp brown paper and string. He wonders if he should tear off the wrapping and turn on the light, get it over with. No. Not yet. The voice chips at the insides of Fletcher's skull like an ice pick, tap, tap, tap it goes, repetitive and nagging, searching for an exit. Filling in his silences, it grows stronger, louder, clearer, thrashing against the walls of his mind. He demands silence, but the Impostor resists, and he struggles to drown him out. He hums loudly to himself, falls to the floor and hugs his knees. He rocks back and forth, trying to shake the voice out, rattling his head from side to side. Fletcher hopes that it might tumble from his ears and fall screaming to the floor. Real, and finally killable, a tangible mass of flesh and blood that he could literally stomp on with his feet, grinding its gasping corpse into the carpet of his unit.

The Impostor.

Inside.

Outside.

Fletcher listens as the Impostor speaks to him. 'To kill the lie and its light, you must kill yourself.'

Fletcher clamps his hands to his ears and tries to laugh, to outwit the voice and trick the Impostor into submission. But soon tears of anguish stream down his cheeks. For the millionth time, he thinks, he really does want to die. It seems like the only way. There is not enough left of himself to fight it any longer. The Impostor is inside his head. It wants out. They both want out, and Fletcher knows what that means.

Bad things are going to happen.

Fletcher Crumb crawls onto his ratty mattress and presses his thumbs deep into his eye sockets. He sees things that aren't there, that simply couldn't be: a blood-red star, its light carnivorous, merging finally into a sinister grey face. He recognises the face but cannot place it, cannot know its name. Winding pathways spill from its daggered, grinning mouth. They branch out into blue nerve-like tentacles, each without end. Two pink stained eyes peer back at him, suspended as if by pulsing electrical cables in the infinite darkness behind his own eyes. Fletcher bashes his head against the floor, rhythmically, in time with the ticking of a wall clock that he thought he had smashed to pieces eons ago. Nope. Tick tock, tick tock it goes, like a bomb that has forgotten how to explode.

Fletcher drifts off to sleep, eventually, and he dreams and kills still more.

He wakes the next morning and immediately decides that he cannot control it any longer. He gets up from the floor and walks towards the door. It has been several days since he has braved daylight and it is time, he decides, to finally let the thing inside him loose. He'll either try to outrun it or it will try to outrun him. Fletcher doesn't know any more. The Impostor is now everywhere. It is complete. Hiding from the myriad images and their lies is no longer feasible. He is hopeful that if he can make it to the butcher shop in the Moralpanik Mall he will know what to do. He has not been there in a while, and he feels consumed by hunger. He knows the Impostor will show himself, leering at him from the montage of glass windows and mirrors that litter the surrounding stores. He fights back the panic as he descends the stairway. He knows that if he braves the outside world, night or day, the cult of his fragmentation will almost certainly overcome him.

Not this time, he thinks, not this time.

He fights with himself to remain calm, walking in brisk but

irregular strides down the footpath. But his steps are over calculated and become more like carefully restrained leaps. Fletcher presses his arms tightly to his sides rather than swing them in time with his legs. It is a tactic he employs to avoid the wild and seemingly uncontrollable hand gestures that characterise his panic attacks. He clamps his jaw closed like a vice and twists the corners of his mouth upwards into a forced smile. It is his public face, an attempt at being inconspicuous and appearing happy go lucky. But the frozen grin and unblinking stare make him appear deranged rather than benevolent.

Locals step quickly aside to avoid colliding with his determined path. An elderly lady with dyed purple hair holds her handbag close to her breast, and narrowly escapes being bowled over. Two young boys, playing on the edge of a park, stop their game and point at him, laughing, thinking him odd and strangely animated.

The manifestation of the Impostor – the twisted and macabre creature that passes itself off as his image – begins to overwhelm him. Fletcher is suddenly aware of a darting shadow, throwing itself over walls and onto the cracked concrete pathway, following him. His breathing becomes irregular, and he talks to himself out loud, striving for affirmations. He succeeds only in scattering gibberish and spittle into the air. The frantic self-assurances do little to anaesthetise his escalating sense of fear. The voice is not his own, he decides. It is the Impostor, reinterpreting his words and strangling his logic.

A bus of schoolgirls watches in awe as Fletcher Crumb screams at the top of his lungs and attempts to outrun his own shadow. The dark, twisting shape sprawls out behind him, and the sunlight is caught in his eyes, so he turns and runs backwards as fast as he can. That way he can keep his eye on the Impostor as it pursues him, he thinks, and hopefully he can lose him before he gets to the mall.

Stubborn objects block his path and refuse to move out of the way. He collides with a phone booth, and then a drinking fountain, in quick succession, and he falls to the ground. Each time he leaps to his feet and continues to run backwards. The light changes again, and he flees down an alleyway and the shadow disappears, breaking into formless fragments that shimmer against the walls. Fletcher turns round and slows his pace to a jog. He stops and looks around, noticing that there appears to be someone else in the alley. Fletcher leans against the wall to catch his breath. He uses his peripheral vision to scope the stranger without staring or drawing undue attention to himself.

The stranger is sitting against the wall and appears to be drinking. Fletcher can smell alcohol and guesses that the stranger is probably a street urchin, and that this alleyway is conceivably his home for now. He's probably harmless, and Fletcher wonders if he should offer him some money. He checks his pockets and realises he has some loose change, but that he left his wallet back at his unit.

The stranger coughs and splutters, and then calls out to him. 'Hey? Hey, mister?' he slurs, urging Fletcher to come closer.

Fletcher slowly walks down the alleyway. It gets darker with every step. He can feel the Impostor moving within him now, crawling under his skin and all over the walls in his mind, mirroring his movements as he approaches the man. He notices a shard of light coming from above, illuminating parts of the wall and the hand of the homeless man and the bottle of wine he is drinking from.

'Want a taste?' the stranger asks.

Realising he is being offered a drink, Fletcher immediately feels more at ease. The stranger looks up and Fletcher sees into his eyes, which are light blue and bloodshot.

The stranger motions for him to take the bottle, holding it aloft. 'It's not a bad drop for the price,' he says, sounding genuinely keen to share.

Fletcher tentatively takes the bottle from the stranger's outstretched hand and notices that he is smiling. He is missing a tooth and has a thick shock of red hair on his head and a rash of uneven stubble.

'Thanks,' Fletcher says, not certain if he should take a sip. He reaches into his pocket with his other hand and grabs at some change.

'There's no charge,' the stranger says. 'I don't want yer money, mister. Just thought you looked like you needed a taste.'

'Oh, sorry,' Fletcher says, letting the change rattle back into the bottom of his pocket.

'Who you running from?' the stranger asks.

'Um… I don't know exactly.'

'Ah, I know the feeling,' he says, laughing and baring his toothless grin.

Fletcher feels even more at ease now, and he raises the bottle to his lips and takes a gulp. It tastes thick and syrupy but not at all as sweet as he expected. He puts it back to his lips and takes another swig.

'That's right, mister, you have yourself a good drink. You'll soon feel better,' the stranger says merrily, not at all concerned that Fletcher is now enthusiastically helping himself to the contents of his bottle.

'What sort of wine did you say this is?' Fletcher asks, now uncertain exactly what it is he can taste.

'Dry red. I think. I don't know for certain…'

'This isn't wine!' Fletcher exclaims in alarm. 'It's blood!'

'Hey?'

'This is blood! Admit it, you've just offered me a drink of blood,' he says wildly.

'What? It's wine. Dry red, mister. I swear!'

'How do you know me?' Fletcher says angrily.

'We just met, mister. Are you crazy?'

'What did this come from?'

'What the hell are you talking about?'

'Listen carefully,' Fletcher clearly exclaims, 'I asked you what… this…came…from!'

'Um…grapes?' the stranger guesses.

'Is it human? Ohhhh nooo… It is!'

'Hang on,' the stranger says, shaking his head in confusion, 'so you're asking me if my wine is human?'

'This is blood!' Fletcher yells. 'Here, taste it!' He thrusts the bottle back into the man's hand.

The stranger is now a bit suspicious. 'Well, I'm not sure I want to now,' he says warily.

'Why? You were drinking it just before, weren't you?'

'Well, it wasn't blood then.'

'Ahh haaaa!' Fletcher says, pointing at the man as if he has just caught him out. 'Sso you finally admit it. It is human blood!'

'How did you turn my perfectly nice bottle of wine into blood?'

'It was already fucking blood you…you monster!'

'Hold on there, mister. I'm not the one drinking human blood here. You are.'

'Taste it!' Fletcher continues to insist.

'I don't want to now. You've probably ruined it,' he says, looking worryingly at his half empty bottle.

'I did not! This is human blood and you made me drink it. Admit it!'

'I was just being generous and you go and do this. What's the world coming to?' the stranger frets, wondering why he bothered being so nice in the first place.

Fletcher is suddenly overcome with theories and connections. 'Are they trying to turn me into a vampire? Is the Impostor a vampire sent to make me drink its blood in order to completely over take my humanity and… Wait, is it my blood? No, it can't be. Unless this stranger is actually a vampire…and he wants me to join his evil coven filled with other rampantly vampiric vampire vamps that suck and kill and… Oh shit…'

Fletcher's mind reels as he finally realises something: this blood is delicious. He can still taste it on his lips. Fletcher feels fantastic, strong and sharp and focused, completely different than before. It is like he just knocked back some superpowered miracle energy drink and the effects are only just kicking in.

'Give me that!' he says, snatching back the bottle and taking another long drink.

'Hey, that's mine!' the stranger says, disappointed, and now wondering if he does want his bottle back after all. Then a thought occurs to him. 'I'm on television, aren't I?' he says, craning his neck to see if he can see any cameras. 'Is this a reality television show, mister?' he asks hopefully. 'Did I win anything?'

But Fletcher is no longer listening. He stops before he finishes the bottle, deciding that he will take it with him and he will have some left for later. The cork is on the ground and he snatches it up, corking the bottle and sliding it under his arm.

'Mister? Mister? Did I win anything?' the stranger continues to ask, wondering when the prank will be revealed and he can savour his new-found but probably temporary fame.

'No,' Fletcher says, looking down and now grinning wickedly at the stranger, 'but I think I just did.'

Without saying another word, Fletcher strides off into the streets and into Moralpanik oblivion, marvelling at his new-found sense of power, grace and clarity. As he picks up his pace, darting and weaving through the urban sprawl, he once more thinks of the Lucidity Le Grande, the mirror of mirrors, waiting for him at home.

The stranger, realising he's probably not the winner of some fantastically wacky reality television show and that his bottle of wine – or maybe blood (he's not sure which now) – has just been stolen by a very strange man indeed, curses to himself. He struggles to get up and ambles down the alleyway in vain pursuit of the far quicker thief. 'Hey, mister! Bring me back my…um…?' he half shouts, not certain any more exactly what has just been stolen from him. That weird guy certainly seemed to like it, though, he thinks. He cheered right up after he drank a bit of it, seemed like he needed a pick-up too.

The stranger wonders if he has enough money for another bottle and decides that if he does, he is going to ask for the exact same wine as last time. Hopefully the checkout lass will remember him. Maybe the word blood appears on the label somewhere, he hopes, in the small type or even in the brand name. It was obviously a fantastic bargain, probably a rare and very well aged drop. If the lass from the bottle-shop can't remember, he'll just ask for a fine bottle of human blood. That should clear things up completely.

Later that afternoon, Fletcher Crumb climbs the steps to the second floor and unlocks the door to Unit 12. He stumbles into the calculated darkness of his home and thinks immediately of the package. He goes directly into his bedroom. His mind is blank and formless, his lips wet. The remainder of the bottle trickles down his chin and stains his jugular and shirt, lingering in his mouth and tantalising him.

He soon finds the package in the corner and immediately begins to tear off its wrapping. Fletcher flings shreds of paper into the air, and they fall from his bedroom sky like invisible rain. Running his hands over it for the first time, the Lucidity Le Grande feels wintry and smooth. Its edges are impossibly detailed and embedded with glass stones. Fletcher leans it against the dark wall and stands in front of it. If the brochure was accurate, this mirror will pardon his every flaw, and that includes the Impostor. 'Absolute Clarity or your Money Back – Guaranteed,' it said. Fletcher braces himself for the revelation of his true self, sans the transience of his imperfections. His left hand reaches out to the dusty wall fixture and he finally turns on the overhead light.

What he sees there in the mirror is not a monster. It is not vile or ugly, nor is it beautiful, as he had secretly hoped. No. The revelation, and the improbable truth of his reflection, is more alarming than real. The Impostor has disappeared. The Impostor that for so long denied his certainty, the cruel being that terrified, tortured and reviled him is suddenly gone. Fletcher Crumb looks deep into the Lucidity Le Grande and sees something he has never seen in a mirror before.

Nothing.

He sees nothing but the room that surrounds him. He sees nothing of himself and his blood-streaked mouth. The mirror looks straight through him, capturing neither his face nor figure. The mirror seems to be unaware he is there at all, rendering him nebulous and absent. The lie and the tortured light offer no reflection, nothing in return, nothing to recognise or reject. The Impostor is gone, and in its place stands something far more frightening.

No one.

Suddenly there is a small spark and a crackle of electricity from above. The light bulb fizzles out, blanketing Fletcher in sudden darkness. He feels nauseous and sways uneasily on his feet. A dreadful sadness washes over him, enveloping his sense of bewilderment and triggering his urgency. Fletcher digs his fingernails deep into the layers of newspaper and glue that mat the bedroom window and he soon tears a hole in the darkness. A shard of daylight stabs his cheek and spills across his shoulder and he recoils in agony. His legs give way and he crumbles to the floor, whimpering. A strangled shriek leaps from his throat, a sound so peculiar, so strangely familiar, that Fletcher Crumb knows that it could only be his own. And then the tears…his own impalpable tears well up like forbidden light in his eyes.

He lies there for hours on the floor, absorbing the majesty of his revelation. The day bleeds into the night. In the inexplicable space between worlds, Fletcher becomes aware of a noise. Something stirs beneath him. The subtle vibrations swell in sound and intensity. Voices become clear and take form in his ears. It is an argument. He has heard it a thousand times before. The two voices battle to be heard, cursing over the top of each other like imperfect echoes of petty conflict, bickering over the last mindless scraps of logic. His inconsiderate neighbours, George and Tiffany Best, are once again invading Fletcher's sense of delirium.

He grits his teeth, waiting for the argument and his rising irritation to subside. When it doesn't, and he feels he can stand it no longer, he bashes the floor with his fists and bellows, 'Will you pleeeaasssse… Just… Shut… Up!'

There is a stunned silence, a momentary lapse in the conflict. And then, as if he had not spoken at all, the voices continue to bicker. Fletcher has had enough. He decides that he will finish this once and for all. He licks at the wetness on his lips and decides he wants some more. Calmly and without hesitation, he leaves his unit and climbs down the flight of stairs and knocks firmly on their door.

A young woman appears in the doorway, wearing a dowdy pink dressing gown and slippers. 'What? What do you want?' she snaps at Fletcher, regarding him with careless disdain.

Her expression is crude and indignant. He regards her hazel eyes, searching for his reflection in a dilated pupil, still looking for the Impostor. He sees no one. Nothing. He lowers his eyes, lingering on the supple white nape of her neck and what lies beneath. A thrill of hunger passes through him. He says nothing.

'Well, what do you want?' she inquires again, annoyed at the inconvenience of the visit.

Fletcher is just about to answer her question, to ravenously sink his teeth deep into her flesh and shut her and her inconsiderate husband up for good, but something unexpected stops him. An abrupt rumbling of thunder and then a flash of lightning echoes through the air. Fletcher Crumb looks suddenly and wistfully into the night, looking for the mouth in the sky, wondering if it will finally open its jaws and drown the world. He is once again the storm, beautiful and violent. He stares like that for some moments, as if searching for a distant place, somewhere beyond imagining. But all that Fletcher sees are stars…stars that have died many light years ago, and whose tortured glow is all that remains.

'What the fuck do you want?' the woman snaps again, clearly out of patience.

'Looks like it might rain,' says Fletcher knowingly, and he grins wickedly at the woman, ever so slightly baring his teeth.

The woman wonders if she should step past Fletcher and look to the sky herself, just to see if this mythical rain is indeed about to manifest, but she decides against it. It is highly unlikely, she decides. It never rains in Moralpanik. Besides, something about the man blocking the doorway dissuades her from further investigation. Perhaps it is the glint of depraved mischief in his eyes. It suddenly seems as if he is capable of anything.

'You'd better stay inside,' Fletcher smirks lasciviously, disarming her with his neighbourly concern,

'I've got a feeling we're in for quite a downpour.'

Just Visiting

Mary's eyes are streaked with tears and dark eyeliner trickles across her pale cheek bones. She sits at the kitchen table and grips Pewter Jesus in her clenched fist. The smiling messiah that she liberated from the bonds of his own cross is now more than just her lucky charm, he is an unlikely friend and confidant. At least it feels that way to Mary. She wonders if he can sense the troubled thoughts that she sends his way.

Jesus, for the first time without his cross, carefully regulates each pewter breath, straining to see deep into Mary's eyes from between the knuckles of her hand. It's not that he is afraid of being crushed to death, he's just concerned. He owes Mary a debt of gratitude but has no idea how to help her. It saddens him to see her so upset, so fragile and beautiful all at once, so lost.

This is Pam's house. Everything in this house belongs to Pam and she often fantasises about telling people as much. Even the sweaty garlic flavoured air is all Pam's, as she sees it, and she'd much prefer that visitors ask for her permission to breathe it. But she doesn't ask that, no, she just thinks it. She dwells upon the unfairness of such uninvited social invasions – Mary, for instance – and tries to think of still more passive-aggressive coping strategies to unleash upon the world. Mary's former step-mother – she was married to Mary's father for a brief time – is currently in self-imposed exile. Pam has locked herself in the bathroom and is chugging on a bong, eating almost-ready-to-turn-and-poison-her French onion dip. It has more bite and character that way, vintage, like foetid cheese. She scoops it straight from the tub with her stubby, nailbitten fingers, in between wacky-weed hits. She will probably toss several pills down her gullet afterwards, just to remain chilled, to level out the paranoia and to muffle her overwhelming sense of resentment. Besides, it's easier to do fake-nice when she's high, more convincing too, and getting fucked up is the only way she knows how to cope.

Nigel will know what to do, Pam thinks, sucking another hit of sweet smoke into her lungs and holding it there. He'll have some money. He always has money for Mary when she needs it. The selfish prick won't give her a dime. At least she got the house in the divorce. Nigel can keep his fall-apart-at-the-seams daughter and the bloody dogs. Pam doesn't care any more.

Why does Mary insist on complicating Pam's life? Why can't Mary move in with her boyfriend and just deal with life like an adult? She always ends up on her couch, and it is Pam's couch. How is she supposed to watch late night television and masturbate to soapies and fitness infomercials with her pregnant former stepdaughter gatecrashing when any little tiff with her boyfriend blows up in her face? There's no me-time, thinks Pam. There's no furiously-climaxing-to-an-episode-of-Celebrity-Big-Brother with Mary around. Doesn't she ever stop to think of Pam, all sick and lonely and on welfare, only just surviving on what Centre-Slink gives her to live on from one day to the next? It's always about Mary. Even with her ex-husband, it's always Mary this and Mary that. 'Is she going okay? Does she have enough money to eat?' 'Find out for yourself, dickhead!' she feels like saying. 'You take her in for once!'

Pewter Jesus can smell the smoke wafting out from underneath the bathroom door. 'What a strange scent,' he thinks. 'I wonder if it's a giant cigarette she's smoking in there?' It certainly is a pungent and alien aroma. If Jesus could only speak, he would ask Mary what it is, but he suspects she is in too much of a state to bother with little details like that. Maybe he'll find out when Mary loosens her grip on him and Pam comes out of the bathroom. He hopes so. Sometimes it's not easy being patient, even for Jesus. After all, Pam has been in there for an awfully long time.

Mary places Pewter Jesus carefully on the table cloth and wipes at the moisture running from her nostrils. She looks around the room to make certain she is alone and then lightly blows her nose on her dress. Pam probably won't come out of self-imposed marijuana exile until her dad gets there. Mary only comes to Pam's place when her dad is working, which seems to be most of the time. If he isn't on the job, he's at home with his de facto partner Stephanie.

Stephanie is a legal secretary and doesn't seem to think too much of Mary. Stephanie tries to be nice but Mary can tell Stephanie wants her to leave as soon as she gets there. It makes her uncomfortable and it's a weird vibe. Stephanie is too young for her dad, Mary thinks, but they seem to be happy. At least Pam lets her crash on the couch for a few days.

Pretty soon Mary will have to get to a hospital, she figures two weeks or so, but who knows? The precious bun in her oven could pop out any time. She gently strokes Pewter Jesus and notices that the grin on his face is gone. Strange, she thinks; maybe it was never there to begin with.

There is a knock at the door and a tentative 'Hello…?' and Mary's dad, Nigel, clad in his police uniform, appears in the doorway.

Pam bursts out of the bathroom simultaneously, smoke billowing into the kitchen like a tsunami. She asks in a put-on homely tone if anyone would like a cup of tea. She scuttles over to the kettle, eyes bloodshot and half closed, miraculously domestic and former step-motherly all of a sudden. She begins to rattle through the cupboards in slow motion.

Nigel ignores her on principle. He sits down at the far end of the table and kindly fixes his eyes on his daughter. 'What's up?' he asks lightly. 'Haven't seen you in a while.'

Mary struggles not to burst into tears and places her hand over Pewter Jesus to hide him from the eyes of her father.

Jesus thinks Mary is protecting him from the cloud of smoke now filling the room. He has finally caught on to the fact that anyone breathing in that noxious stuff could conceivably transform into Pam, and that wouldn't be a good thing. He holds his breath and counts sacrificial sheep. Every soon-to-be-slaughtered lamb bleats at him unhappily as it leaps over the electrified fence in his mind. He wonders if he's already been infected by the poisonous smog, and at any moment he will pass into some comatose netherworld. It's a place in his mind where every other messiah he encounters swears that they're the chosen one and is possessed of their own cross. And he's the little black sheep of the bunch, cross-less and made of cheap pewter, instead of the divine flesh and blood of a convincing, babblical messiah. A strange sense of panic descends upon Jesus, creeping beneath Mary's hand like holy smoke.

Mary looks up at her father and the tears finally begin to flow. Nigel stands up and moves to where his daughter is sitting. He puts his hand on her shoulder and Mary continues to cry. Her father is giving her permission to not be okay, but she still feels embarrassed to be so openly emotional.

'Let's go for a walk,' her father says. 'It's warm outside...the sun's shining... If you walk a little, you might start feeling better.'

Nigel looks up at Pam, who is pretending not to be off her face and giving a look – completely self-serving of course – that suggests she highly approves of Nigel's walk idea. Mary picks up Jesus and slides him into the side strap of her bra. She follows her father out of the house.

Outside in the warm sun, they stroll side by side down the footpath. Neither of them says a word.

Jesus lies contentedly in Mary's bra strap, glad to be away from the poisonous smog and Pam, who he suspects is some sort of emotional terrorist bent on destroying the world with her evil smoke machine. Pam is most probably a minion of the Anti-Christ, he thinks, if indeed there actually is one. Yes, a housebound lesser demon with shady eating habits. She keeps the diabolical smoke machine in the bathroom and activates it at times just like these. If Mary and her father intend on going back inside the house at any point, he will have to warn them somehow. 'It's not safe in there!' he would holler aloud if he only could. 'The Beast has unleashed the smoke machine of death! Run for your fucking lives!'

Pewter Jesus has heard some swearing in his time, and he would not usually condone it. The word 'fucking' however (whatever that means?), is probably appropriate under these extreme circumstances. The trouble is, Jesus hasn't worked out how to audibly communicate with Mary yet. He suspects that if she were to pray to him at any point, which is entirely plausible, he might find it possible to reply. If she's contemplating going anywhere near that horrendous Joseph fellow again, they really are going to have a serious talk. No, Joseph is a perverted fiend with serious designs on womb-stealing. He wants to liberate Mary's uterus and make a home for himself in there. Whether he would fit is not the point; the moral logistics of such an uninvited invasion are unthinkable. Jesus is having none of it.

Joseph isn't the Christ child's father, thinks Pewter Jesus resolutely. No, the little cherub inside of Mary is the second coming of the Chosen Guy. Or maybe he's the third or fourth or, perhaps, even the seventeenth incarnation of a Chosen Dude? Jesus ponders, the wrinkles in his furrowed pewter brow knotting due to the very deep depths of such a bottomless thought. It's got to be something like that, doesn't it? It's getting hard to discern. How is one supposed to know? There are so many vivid and flamboyant approximations of the Chosen Guy in Moralpanik that trying to weed out the pretenders is impossible. Jesus guesses that he falls into that very category himself; just another messiah among many. They should have a fancy parade once a year for all the Chosen Dudes, he thinks fondly, like the gays do. Pewter Jesus could even have his own float, he thinks. Either that or he'd end up tucked in the sweaty jockstrap of some hard bodied, queer Chosen Dude. He pictures them wildly gyrating up against a giant inflatable crucifix. Ah, the looks of wonderment from the enthralled faithful would be divine. Yes, they could celebrate their sameness and the fact that they are all so different in the exact same way; a lewd parade of dancing Chosen Dudes covered in holy coconut oil and unleavened confetti.

Body of Christ?

Amen.

At the end of the block, Mary and her father stop walking and turn to each other.

'I'm sorry, Dad,' says Mary. 'I'm always doing this, aren't I?'

'That's okay,' Nigel replies, shrugging in affirmation. 'I know I'm not allowed to ask, but is it that guy? You know, the one who did that to you,' he says, pointing awkwardly at her pregnant paunch.

'Uh, yeah... It's um, complicated,' Mary says, unleashing what she knows to be an all-purpose cliché and then looking sadly at her father's shoes.

Mary is still not certain exactly how she became pregnant in the first place. She had been on the pill and she always made Joseph wear a condom, no matter what. Somehow, she got knocked up anyway. Go figure. She'd never slept with anyone else, ever, so it was quite a nightmare to discover she was knocked up at the age of nineteen.

'You can ask, Dad,' Mary continues, 'but I just don't know if I can explain things without you getting angry.'

'Does he hit you?' Mary's father asks, irate and flustered, fulfilling Mary's prophecy immediately. 'If I find out that fucker has ever hit you... I don't know what I'll do,' he seethes angrily.

'No, Dad, he doesn't hit me,' Mary replies, not certain if she is telling the truth or not. Joseph has done some strange things around Mary, but she's not sure they were technically considered to be abuse.

'He...loves me,' she stammers, now on the defensive. 'At least...I think he does?' she then wonders silently to herself.

'For fuck's sake, Mary! He doesn't act like it,' her father continues, now on a roll. 'I swear, every time I see you like this,' he spits, again waving his finger bluntly at Mary's belly and then the mess of make-up smeared across her otherwise pretty face, 'I just wanna track the bastard down and crack his fucking head open!'

'I left *him* this time, Dad, so you don't need to get all crazy.'

'Okay,' he says, holding his hands up, agreeing to back off. 'Okay…that's strong of you…that's good,' he says, now warming to the idea that his daughter can stand up for herself.

'I just need time to think, Dad. I don't even know if he's really… you know…' she says, her voice trailing off. 'I'm not sure he'll make the most stable father for the child,' she thinks of saying, but decides against it. No, her father would not understand.

'Don't go back to the guy. It really is that easy,' he says, now resolute. 'He' is wrong for you Mary, why can't you see that?'

'You don't even know him, Dad,' Mary replies.

Unfortunately, she can picture what it would be like if Joseph and her father did meet, and she knows without a doubt that it would be a disaster. Joseph is far too out there, and her father is way too overprotective of her, and he has a wicked temper and a very short fuse. If Joseph introduced himself as Super-Duper-Man, which was likely, her father would probably punch his lights out immediately. Joseph's imagined super powers would be all for nought. In fact, Mary's father would probably then lift his limp body up off the ground by the neck of his little red cape and continue to pummel Super-Duper-Man into a permanent coma.

Things with her father are getting way too intense, too serious. Mary feels the need to diffuse the tension somehow.

'Oh…poor me, whatever shall I do?' Mary asks sarcastically, holding the back of her hand up to her brow, intentionally mocking herself.

Despite her meaning the question to be rhetorical, her father answers anyway. 'You can stay with me…with Stephanie and me.'

'No, I can't, Dad,' Mary snaps back, infuriated at her father's insistence that they continue along the same path.

'Why the hell not, Mary? I swear, sometimes you're so goddamn stubborn!'

'Yes, Dad… I get it from you,' she retorts, now deadpan.

'You can't do this on your own, you know,' he insists.

Mary is silent for a moment, soaking her situation in, then her eyes well with tears all over again. 'You don't understand. You can't. I need to do this on my own. I have to go my own way,' she continues, and then realises suddenly that they have both had enough, 'I don't want to talk about it any more.'

'But we need to talk this out, Mary.'

'End of con-ver-sat-ion!' Mary declares emphatically. She holds the palm of her hand up to signal that the exchange between them, at least for now, is over.

The two of them go silent, but after a while Mary softens, knowing her father means well, and she punches him affectionately on the arm. Still upset but putting on a brave face, she says, 'I'll figure it out. It'll be fine. Pam should let me crash for a few days and I've got an appointment with Centre-Slink tomorrow. Maybe they can help set me up or something, the single mother's pension might be the way to go.'

'All right...' Nigel says with a sigh of resignation. 'I can help you out with a few hundred for now.'

'Thanks, Dad... I'll owe you...'

They walk back towards the house, quietly side by side.

Pewter Jesus, who has of course been listening in the entire time, has just realised they are going back into the polluted den of iniquity Pam calls a home. He screams out in panic, 'Nnnnnnoooooooooooooo ooooooooooooooooo!'

Unfortunately for Jesus, his desperate attempt to sound the alarm amounts to little but a courageous display of unheard and bra strap muffled protest.

Mary and her father continue back towards the house anyway, unaffected and unaware of the impending horror that Jesus is certain awaits them.

'Now we're really stuffed...' Jesus groans in silent defeat. 'Ab-so-lute-ly fucked!'

Magpies

Is it possible to laugh oneself to death? Is it possible to literally laugh one's head off?

Such are the questions you ask yourself as you leave the asylum, for after a five-year stretch in an institution that was designed to break you, you are finally free. You await the arrival of the Greyhound bus that will take you back into the city. You rehearse canine jokes in your head, standing outside the ominous gates that have opened just for you. Finally, released back into the wild: the laughter-starved world outside of the asylum.

Your early release is due to a particularly well organised and overwhelmingly consensual effort on behalf of the inmates and all the staff to get you the hell out of there. It worked. You were released on the condition you would keep your sordid jokes to yourself. You have no such intentions, of course, but you suspect they all know that.

While inside, you refused to play along, mercilessly mocking and lampooning all and sundry with your rapier-like wit. It is your firm belief now that you were simply too funny for them to comprehend. People laugh later, you always tell yourself; they fall into hysterics after the fact. It is this firm, unshakable belief that keeps you comically relevant. No laughter means automatic miscomprehension; silence means the inability to interpret ironies so cleverly ironical that they almost always mean that the opposite of opposite is in direct opposition to the opposing irony.

In truth, most people just don't get your jokes straight away. They act offended and hurt, assuming you are a cruel and heartless man. When they have had time to think and absorb the majesty of your gags

– after a torrent of well-honed comic lacerations have left all of those within earshot bleeding and writhing on the floors in agony – only then do they laugh, afterwards, when you are long gone. That is when they finally see the funny side. Yes, then the gathered minions of your laugh-delay-plagued audience erupt into rapturous applause.

You have rarely experienced laughter in person. You have seldom been in its presence. The laughter always comes later, when you are absent. In the asylum, they failed to realise this. So documents got signed and unsigned, and the rules and legislation of the place of your incarceration were manipulated and scandalously broken. They were sick of your constant and unabated streams of foolhardy cruelty, they said. Your sense of humour is what got you in there and, once inside, it also got you out. And for only five years of a ten-year grammatically incorrect sentence no less.

The humourless judge who put you away was deeply offended by your vivid and colourful description of his legally bound third testicle. You described it being hammered into submission with the very gavel he used to silence your earlier impersonation of an aroused ferret, sniffing at his dangly bits. Knowing full well it too was in grave danger of passing out from the rancid belching of the judge's blabbering bottom, and the unnecessarily complicated legal jargon that seeped from it into the courtroom. It was a brilliant enough spiel to get you a ten-year sentence. The aroused ferret in question is still at large.

You currently have no parole officer, nor legal representation, as no one will take your case. You are free, yet cursed you remain. For you lust for immediate recognition, for the instantaneous and glory-bound echoes of cackling laughter; the reward for your infinitely clever yet misinterpreted witticisms. There is no doubt in your mind that you are a stand-up comedian. You tell people this while you are sitting down. They look at you with a quizzical unease, tilting their heads, waiting for further elaboration. You give them none, always waiting for the unfathomable penny to drop. The world is just not in on the joke yet, but they will cotton on. Oh yes, you just pray that it happens before it is too late. A funny man should be a wealthy man, not a dead one. You fear for your life. Modern scientists will want to scoop out your brains and analyse them, searching for the profound secret to your comic genius. Murderous comedians will conspire to kill you out of envy, wanting to put an end to your hilarious, scene-stealing dominance over the soon to be laughing world.

You exit the Greyhound bus noisily, barking at the driver. Drool splashes on his raised arms and face as you yap and snap at him; itching at invisible fleas. You attempt to hump his leg but he is having none of it, and he angrily waves you away. As the door closes behind you, your ears detect a wave of laughter, a familiar merriment of the time-delayed variety. 'Who was that guy?' The passengers must be thinking. 'How can all that mirth fit within just one man?' And those questions again: 'Is it possible to laugh oneself to death? Is it possible to literally laugh one's head off? If one can, then this guy is a potential serial killer, a mass murderer, a black comedy plague,' they are surely thinking.

You read their thoughts out loud, as the snickering bus rocks from side to side-splitting side, fading into the distance.

You should probably make your way to your allocated but temporary accommodation. It is getting late. If the passengers convince the driver to do a U-turn and come back for you, things could get awkward. They want more, of course; that is understandable, but you don't wish to inconvenience the bus driver. Even if he is a terrible straight guy (he flat out had no comic timing at all), he still has a job to do. He has a family to feed, people are relying on him. You can certainly relate. Yet for you the stakes are much higher, the immense pressure more keenly felt.

The details of your provisional lodgings are written on a piece of crumpled, yellowing paper. You study the address as you make your way down a winding one-way street. The words 'What is your name?' have been scrawled in bold red ink on the other side of the paper. Stranger still, you realise it is a question you simply cannot answer.

Who are you?

When you arrive at the boarding house, you are fatigued; it was a long walk.

A hairy, middle-aged man with shifty eyes and a startling mono brow greets you at the door. He says all the following without moving his lips: 'Greetings, Earthling, my name is Zeus, God of Exclusion. You must be that comedian everyone is talking about. Yes, that's you. You're all over the television and the internet. Yes, the funny guy, funniest guy ever, and very famous indeed. Loved by basically everyone you are. Oh, except other comedians that is. But we all know why that is, don't we? In fact, it's obvious to everyone but you,' He blathers on and on.

You are taken aback. You didn't expect this. You follow him inside and you are suddenly in a communal kitchen. He produces a stack of papers and hands you a pen. He obviously wants your autograph.

'Okay, Zeus, where do I sign?' you say humbly, taking the adulation in stride.

You scribble something resembling an autograph on the papers and he hands you some keys.

He grunts and then continues to blather on about you without moving his lips. 'They're planning on making a film about your life except you'll be playing with yourself – sorry, you'll be playing the part of yourself, yourself – and there are rumours that there will be microphones and tracking devices embedded in your teeth and your arse, and cameras in your breakfast cereal in order to capture every breath, but if you have any demands, by all means talk to the director and she'll see what she can do, because we all love you except you-know-who, and everything rests on whether the audience is still alive enough at the end of filming for us to begin the process of torturing the truth out of them. So, if no one laughs, just go with it. We've covered all the bases and we have a plan for you. The shitter is out the back if you need to go.'

You now suspect he is a deranged ventriloquist, but you don't want to make him feel self-conscious, so you say nothing of it. He leads you to your dressing room and you whisper that he should come inside, at least briefly, as you have important questions to ask.

'Psssst,' you hiss, 'are there any types here that I should know about, Zeus?'

'It's Mason,' he says, correcting you, except this time his lips are moving, curling around his words.

You shrug at the obvious contradiction. You wonder if his name will continue to change like this. You put your hand in your pocket and retrieve a few coins. You press a shiny fifty-cent piece into his hand and winking, you say, 'You know, undesirables?'

'Like what?' he says, perhaps feigning confusion.

'You know, comedians, entertainers, those types,' you whisper confidentially.

'Ohhhh, those types,' he says nodding emphatically, seeming to finally get it.

Yet he turns and leaves the room without answering your question, he just walks off. How rude, you think. Your bribe should have fetched you more than this. Has the currency of greased-palm-capitalism devalued so much since you were locked away? But then you hear him laugh out loud, an unmistakable flurry of mirth. As you close the door to your dressing room, you realise something: he found your questions amusing, hilarious even. You don't seem to be able to turn off your gift. You weren't even trying to be funny, and yet once again you were a hit with audiences everywhere. What is this curse of yours, you wonder.

You yawn and stretch melodramatically, loudly enough to be heard by everyone in the boarding house. You employ this tactic to dissuade any further visitors keen to dine at the buffet of your comedic gift. You need uninterrupted sleep. Those hungering for more of you than you can give right now will simply have to wait. You lock the door and collapse onto the bed.

Instead of sleeping, you proceed to masturbate furiously. You imagine you are biting the heads off magpies and chasing gay leprechauns, spitting mouthfuls of blood and feathers at them as they flee from you in green Irish terror. You can't remember where you are. You can't remember your name. You suspect you do not have one. You orgasm and scream silently into your pillow, muffling the *petite mort* afterglow.

You sleep unevenly, sweating nervously through your dreams. When you awake in the morning, you are hungry, but you have no need for food, much like you have no need of a name. You console yourself with the knowledge that the cameras are still rolling, and the thought washes over you like a wave of salty ocean froth.

You wander through the streets and linger in public parks, smiling for the cameras hiding in every tree, in every shady glance, in every parked car. You stare at your reflection in coffee shop windows. You marvel at fancy cakes you will never eat. You squint at a bonny waitress's ample bosom, eyeing her neon name tag with envy. They only give name tags to people with names, you think.

You watch people walking in and out of a bank, clutching their wallets and handbags to themselves like dirty secrets, dressed how people who have money dress. You consider robbing the bank to pay for an expensive dress for yourself. It would have to be something floral, a sheer summer frock for dancing with shifty strangers and frolicking through cruel meadows, free and easy, commando style. But you are a comedian, not a transvestite, and the thought of all that low-hanging, fruity freedom makes you nervous. Your palms sweat and your nipples itch. Your mind throbs and your temples burn with searing prayers of true disbelief. You walk on, chatting to unresponsive, snobbish mailboxes and leering at pretty women you will probably never kiss.

You notice a sprinkler in someone's garden and decide you are thirsty. The yard appears to be unoccupied. You leap the fence and dive on the sprinkler as if it were a rabid animal, pissing into the air. Once your thirst is quenched you notice a particularly babblical-looking bush dotted with red flowers. You consider setting it on fire, but you don't want to unnecessarily mock God or Moses.

A fleeting shadow darts by, and you feel air rush past the back of your neck. Angry magpies swoop down and peck at your skull, defending their nests. You are about to run for cover when you notice a stirring at the side door of the house. The residents are making their way into the garden. You decide that these swooping magpies should be a part of the entertainment. You maintain your position on stage. Another two birds swoop down and peck at your skull in quick succession. You do nothing to dissuade them or protect yourself. Instead, you release your belt and let your pants fall to your ankles.

The audience is about to enter the auditorium.

Now, blood is trickling down the base of your neck. You take your noble todger in hand and begin to masturbate heatedly. An elderly man and a younger lady appear in the yard. They look shocked. Both are wearing shiny yellow bike helmets, but there are no bicycles that you can see. Their rather stylish apparel is possibly a tactic they have employed to fend off magpie attacks, you think, but more than likely it is an ill-advised attempt to upstage you.

As they edge carefully closer, you up the ante, masturbating ever more furiously and staring defiantly into their panicked but admiring eyes. The magpies continue to attack. Now, blood is streaming down your face and welling in your eyes. You finally climax. Defiant and spent you blitz, spinning in circles like an amphetamine gobbling merry-go-round, impregnating the well-manicured lawn with your machine-gun seed.

When it is over, you are exhausted, and more than a little dizzy. You struggle to regulate your breathing as the world continues to turn. The two of them just stand there, filled with wonder, staring. You wait for them to laugh or applaud, but still nothing, just dumbfounded stares.

'Are you finished?' the man asks you dryly, swaying yet sarcastic, now a little uneasy on his feet.

You look about you, mayhem on the ground and a war in the sky. Silence abounds when it should not. Diving, bloodthirsty magpies regale you with their unspoken stories, feasting on chunks of your blood, hair and flesh. Are you the butt of some cosmic, inside-joke? Is this a metaphysical aviary?

The audience yawns, stricken with boredom, unconvinced. Perhaps physical comedy is not their thing?

'Knock, knock,' you say, trying a different tack.

The old man doesn't reply. He looks down at your limp todger and grimaces in disgust, shaking his head. Paling before you, he turns to the woman and says, 'Call the police.'

It's obviously a bluff, you think. He's a competitive type and he just lost the big game. It can't be gratifying being upstaged like this. You can understand his consternation, but it is sympathy you can offer him and not empathy. 'I cannot put myself in your shoes as you are currently wearing them,' you think of saying, but it is a lame gag and you decide to leave it unsaid. Having never been in the unenviable position of being 'the upstaged guy', you are unlikely to achieve an empathic expression that is genuine.

It is important to remain true to oneself, you think. No faking. No selling out. No feigning fucking empathy.

'Knock, knock, knock, knock?' you say again more urgently, growing impatient with the old man's refusal to play his part. You understand the joke does not begin with a third or fourth knock, but you throw them in anyway. What the hell, perhaps you can disarm him, tempt him into crossing over to the funny side? Perhaps he will soon die from laughter? No, his head remains perched on his slumped shoulders. Yet he looks paler, weaker than he did. Is that what you want from all of this, death? Is this your killing joke?

Whatever the case, you feel daring and carefree, dangerous even. You are breaking the rules.

Fuck the Man and fuck the System, but don't fuck the fucking Joke.

No. Fuck that.

Realising the performance is basically over, you pull up your pants and do up your belt. The old man is possibly dismayed at this sudden drawing of the curtains, but every matinee must end. Disappointment seeps from the deep lines in his face, framing him as a tragic figure, a man in mourning, wrestling with infinite yet intangible sorrow. Yet you can't allow his maudlin longing for more noble todger time to derail your happy-meal train. The show is over, motherfucker. Get used to it, you think.

You walk back through the sprinkler's discharge and your pants soak up the spray. You notice that a small rainbow has appeared above the water. Yet there are no gay leprechauns to be seen, and there is no more comedy gold to speak of. Instead, at either end of the rainbow lie exhausted magpies, twitching in the death throes, unlikely to fly again. Their black and white feathers absorb the rainbow's iridescent mist. The colour spectrum pulsates for you, like a kinky ghost blanketed in parrot puke. Your blood congeals upon talons and unblinking eyes, like paint drying unwatched, immortalising the scene stealing beaks of your conquerors.

Suddenly, you find that you cannot move, nor can you tear your eyes away. You marvel at the tableau, so terrifyingly beautiful, you think, so infinitely final. It's the potential of it all, see? Like an unread poem or an untold joke or a life unlived. The unkillable comedy reels unravel for you, stretching out forever like singed nerve endings, beyond the impossible horizon, beyond knowable pain. Still, you feel nothing but defeat. The sound of the sirens grows ever louder, drowning your stage, silencing the punch line, undoing all that you have done.

Finally, you can see the funny side. The laughter manifests as a lump in your belly, hiding from the light, but the unhinged cancer soon travels upwards. Filling your chest cage, immersing your lungs and then rising into your throat. You begin to laugh audibly, just snickering at first. But then your jaw spasms open and you guffaw loudly. The laughter takes hold. Your shoulders tremor and your eyes stream with vulgar tears. Soon, the laughter morphs into a hacking cough and punchlines scatter the air before your eyes. A sharp pain surges up your spine and repeatedly jackknifes you in the back of the neck. The laughter grows so loud you fear your eardrums will explode. Something has to give.

Then it happens: your head completely dislodges from between your shoulders, launching into the air like a popped cork, leaving your body far behind. You leave with it, tumbling onto the grass in a series of dull thuds. You roll to an awkward standstill beneath a nearby tree. Your severed neck bleeds on an exposed root, painting it with pained mirth. You are just a head now, you think, a decapitated nut, separate from your torso and limbs. As this new world revolves around you, you realise you can still see through your eyes. You look through the filaments of your jellied pupils, peering into the yard. Your body is a few feet away from your new locale, headless, defiant, still standing bolt upright in the middle of the garden. Blood pisses from the gaping hole between your shoulders, squirting into the sky like a stuttering fountain. It weeps over your chest and chequered shirt.

You can vaguely make out two figures in the background. The old man has collapsed. His body lies motionless on the grass. The young lady crouches over him, shaking him by the shoulders, attempting to rouse him in vain.

'Help!' she screams out to no one in particular, sobbing in desperation. 'He's not breathing!'

You manage a curiously moist smile, watching bemused as your headless body turns and begins to walk away. Stepping lithely over the dead man on the ground, and careful not to further disturb his distraught companion, it leaps swiftly over the garden fence. Without a care in the world, it merrily skips off down the street.

'Don't leave me!' you consider crying out, but you decide against it. No, things are better this way, you think.

Your eyelids feel suddenly heavy, weighed down by the burden of your vanishing kingdom. The scene blackens, consumed by a tide of creeping ink. The curtains close and a distant audience reluctantly applauds. You bow inelegantly in the gathering darkness, regaled by sweet waves of distorted laughter. Cold hands reach out and pull you under. The laughter fades into less than nothing.

Without so much as a snivelling whimper, you are dragged forever away.

Fans

A small green car pulls into the Moralpanik Ministry Asylum's car park; the engine of the old rust-bucket Beamer splutters to a standstill. A frail thin sixty-year-old woman steps out of the driver-side door. Varicose veins streak the bony lower legs that peak out from beneath her matronly grey dress. She turns to retrieve a black handbag and a birthday cake. It is covered in cling wrap and sits on a ceramic dinner plate. She then slams the door shut with a swift nudge of her hip. She doesn't bother locking the door or rolling up the half open window. The car is not worth stealing and there is nothing of value to be found in its cramped interior. She strides purposefully towards the wrought-iron gate that leads through to the shrubbery and faded flowers that dot the outer yards of the asylum. As usual, the grounds are immaculately still and unoccupied, pruned to an eerily lifeless perfection.

Gladys Slattery presses a button beside the gate and talks into the speaker. 'Miss Slattery to see Joseph Slattery,' she says, smiling into the camera eye above the gate.

'Do you have a passss, Missss Sssslattery?' a female voice inquires.

'Um, yes, somewhere here,' Gladys replies, balancing the cake under her arm and rummaging through her handbag. 'I hope I didn't forget it, I'm so forgetful sometimes,' she frets. 'Ah yes, here we are,' she says, holding the small rectangular card up to the camera.

'Could you please ssswipe it through the sssslot, Missss Ssslattery?'

'Oh, yes that's right,' she says breathlessly, 'and, heavens above, I was only here just the other day!'

She swipes the card and the gate grinds open. Gladys ambles

through to the first set of doors and enters the main reception area of the asylum. There are a few people milling about, but the main reception desk itself is free for the moment. Gladys approaches the two secretarial staff sitting behind the desk. Their faces are made up with thick layers of dark red, black and white oily make-up. Their eyes are small and pitch-black, peering out from behind the glass separating them from Gladys, like those of two snakes poised to strike.

'What can I do for you, madam?' the reptile on the left asks in a polite but cold tone.

'I'm here to see my son, Joseph Slattery. I was here just the other day. I forget exactly which day. It's his birthday today and I just thought I'd bring him this cake,' Gladys says, adding, 'He shouldn't really be in here, you know, he really is a very good boy.'

'Let me jussst check for you, Misssss Ssslattery, I'll jussst be a moment.' The receptionist types a few words onto the computer keyboard in front of her, and she scans the screen with her lifeless eyes. 'There will be a sssmall wait for you, I'm afraid, Missss Ssslattery. But if you'll jussst follow the elevatorsss on the right up to the fourth floor, you can wait in the lounge area until you are called. There is tea and coffee available, and plenty of magazinesss. I'm ssssured it won't be too long.'

'If I may ask, dear, is my son Joseph still in solitary confinement?' Gladys asks.

'Yesss, he isss. He was injured quite badly jussst before being brought in to the asssylum. We feel he needsss time to calm down and ssseriously think about hisss behaviour…and to recover of courssse. But you know that don't you, Missss Ssslattery? If I recall, you were in here jussst yesssterday,' the receptionist says, smiling slyly. 'You had a cake with you then too.'

The other receptionist then pipes in, also grinning wickedly, 'Hasss poor little Josssseph'sss birthday come around again already, Missss Ssslattery? Why, it feelsss like only yesssterday,' she sneers, feigning politeness but revelling in derision.

Gladys shakes her head and frets again, 'You'd best mind your own business, missy!' she snaps back. Gladys takes a deep breath and holds her head high, trying to regain her composure.

She heads over to the elevators. The doors of one open immediately. A nurse in a white uniform with thick scaly ankles and smeared make up exits the elevator. Gladys tries to engage eye contact and smile kindly, but the nurse rudely brushes past Gladys and she steps into the elevator alone. The doors close. Gladys puts on her spectacles and eyes the buttons on the elevator wall. There are ten. The ninth-floor button has the words 'Messiah Ward' boldly written next to it, the seventh 'Vampire Ward', and the fifth, 'Recreation – Gaming Parlour'. Button four is the one she is looking for. It reads 'Solitary Confinement and Processing'. It lights up in yellow as Gladys presses it. The elevator then slowly launches upwards. It stops as the second-floor button, which reads 'Serial Killers Anonymous', lights up and the doors slide open.

Another nurse enters the lift, pushing an old man in a wheelchair.

'Hello there, madam,' he says welcomingly to Gladys before the doors have a chance to close.

He outstretches his hand and Gladys shakes it, glad that finally someone is being genuinely friendly. The nurse continues to stare blankly ahead.

'Are you here to visit someone?' the wheelchair-bound man asks.

'Why yes, I'm here to visit my son, Joseph,' she replies.

'Which section is he in, if you don't mind me asking?'

'He's in Solitary Confinement. They're processing him, whatever that means. And then hopefully he can come home with me so I can look after him,' she says, warming to the old man's chatty demeanour.

'I think you'll find your son's stay here at the asylum will be longer than you think, I'm afraid,' he says.

'Why do you say that?'

Before the old man can answer, the elevator suddenly stops moving, coming to a halt between floors. The mechanical engine powering the cables shudders to a standstill and the metal walls around them rattle.

'Oh, that'sss jussst great,' the nurse curses in anguish. She reaches for the buttons and starts pressing them all, clearly irritated by the suddenly malfunctioning lift.

'Don't worry,' the old man says, leaning towards Gladys and ignoring the nurse, 'this happens all the time. These lifts are very old and they sometimes just take a while to get going. It shouldn't be too long before Maintenance fixes the problem,' he reassures her. 'May I be so bold as to ask your name, madam?' he asks courteously.

'Oh…no, of course not,' she replies. 'I'm Gladys. Gladys Slattery. What's yours?'

'You may call me Captain,' he says smiling.

'Oh, and what are you a captain of…Captain?'

'Nothing really, Gladys. That's just what they call me around here. I've been here for a very long time. What started out as a nickname just sort of stuck. I like it. It makes me feel a little more important than I probably am,' he says frankly.

'So, why are you in here, in this asylum… Are you mentally… um… you know?' Gladys says, fumbling for the right words so as not to be presumptuous or appear unnecessarily rude.

'I'm from floor nine, the Messiah Ward as they call it. It's for patients who have babblical identity issues…or delusions of babblical grandeur as the nursing staff here most crudely term them. You may have noticed that I just exited the Serial Killers Anonymous Ward. There's no need to worry, though,' Captain stresses, most unnecessarily. 'I go where I'm most needed. I know a few troubled souls that I tend to in there. I myself can leave the asylum any time I wish. I just choose not to.'

Gladys regards Captain with wide-eyed curiosity, regaled by his charming banter and openly engaging manner. 'Why? Do you like it here?' she asks, intrigued.

'Not particularly, Gladys. It's okay. I just feel I'm needed here, to help guide some of the patients, to make them feel they have a fighting chance of getting out. I consider it my responsibility, as any truly good person would in my position.'

The nurse, who has been on the elevator's emergency phone calling for Maintenance to fix the problem, interrupts their conversation. 'Oh, do ssshut up, Captain! The Ssserial Killer Ward issss where you belong. You're jussst asss crazy asss any of the other lunaticsss in here.'

'Lies! Don't listen to this reptile, Gladys!' Captain says boldly. 'She's like all the other staff, a rude and controlling snake! What is your son's apparent malady?' Captain inquires, eager to quickly shift the emphasis away from the nature of his own predicament.

'He thinks he is – or he really is, I'm not completely certain which – a superhero. He calls himself Super-Duper-Man. But he really is a good boy. He shouldn't be in here. I could look after him at home. I want to anyway, but he's always running off and getting into trouble.'

'Ahhhh…he'll probably end up in the Superhero Ward then, see…' Captain says, pointing at the tenth-floor elevator button, which actually has 'Superhero Ward' written next to it.

'Oh my…no…no, that won't do at all! They can't put him in there, especially in a place like this,' Gladys frets.

'Oh, you needn't worry about the Superhero Ward. They're a lovely bunch, if occasionally a bit on the psychotic, comic-book violence side. No, what you really need to worry about with your son are the machines.'

'What do you mean, Captain? What are the machines?'

'The Medication Mind-Blitz Machines. Just about everyone in here ends up strapped to them at some point. They get hooked, hypnotised, and then they can't stop playing them. Problem is, you can't win. I know from personal experience. They're evil, the Mind-Blitz Machines. They're very, very bad for everyone. The nurses will tell you it's the only way to get better and to eventually be let out of here, to be free. What they don't tell you is that until you've been turned into a vegetable, or a shadow of your former self by those damnable machines, they won't let you leave! If you really love him, and I can tell you do, whatever you do don't let him go anywhere near the machines. He'll find them fun at first but…but…ooooh shit –' Captain's line of conversation goes suddenly silent and his eyes roll into the back of his head. His face slumps groggily onto his chest.

Gladys notices that the nurse has just jammed a large needle into the side of his neck and pumped him full of some nasty-looking black liquid.

'Oh my…' Gladys gasps in shock. 'What did you have to do that for?' she asks. 'We were just chatting!'

'You lisssten to me, Missss Ssslattery, and take heed. Thiss Captain, asss he callss himself, may seem like a nicccce old man to you but he'sss cccertainly not. Captain isss a delusional troublemaker and a dangeroussss lunatic. If I were you, Gladyssss!' the nurse says, poking her finger sharply and with considerable force into Gladys's sternum, 'I wouldn't bother taking anything that he sssaid too ssseriously. In fact, I highly recommend you forget everything he just sssaid and go on your way without making a fusssssssss!' she warns ominously, hissing and spraying Gladys with her spittle.

The elevator suddenly begins to rattle into motion again and continues its ascent towards the next floor. Gladys shakily steps out when the doors finally open on the Solitary Confinement and Processing level of the Moralpanik Ministry Asylum, feeling quite spooked and more than a little upset.

As the doors close behind Gladys Slattery, the reptile, chortling on as if the heated warning and vicious jab in the chest did not occur, cheerfully says, 'You have a nicccccce vissssssssit now, Missss Ssslattery… and a glorioussssssss day!'

*

Joseph watches the door keenly, studying the shadow that bleeds across it with a mingling of expectation and awe. He arches his back and

115

doubles his grip, straining to remain focused and calm, concentrating intently on the task at hand: hanging from the ceiling fan.

Apart from the green tissue-paper crown on his head and a luminous pair of ridiculously tight red bathers, Joseph is naked. Feeling a cruel inner chill, he shudders endlessly, infinitely. A vision of cotton wool clouds and a happily smiling crayon sun fills his head. It is all that he has: an imitation of what it means to be outside. It is his birthday today, and he feels certain that his guests will be impressed by the surprise he has in store. They will be arriving soon and he is determined to be ready for them.

'What a wondrous sight, what a fabulous party trick,' they will say.

Joseph smiles wickedly as he looks down upon his birthday cake. It smoulders on the floor directly beneath him, its twenty-one candles aflame, ablaze with the promise of his immortal birthday wish. Plates of fairy bread and jelly beans surround the cake, chocolate -bullets and multicoloured popcorn guarding the central motif. Joseph watches over his party spread from above, with both legs wrapped tightly around a steel fan blade. His hands cling to the spine of the fan and his pores weep a clammy sweat. A thick matt of dark body hair snakes across his chest and thins out on his upper back. Tiny beads of perspiration cling to his hair and occasionally break away from it, dripping on the jelly beans and causing them to glisten. They have so far avoided the cake and its candles, because Joseph finds that if he wiggles his upper body, ever so carefully, he can guide the falling droplets away from the flames.

Joseph's eyes are piercing and, in a certain light, almost nefarious. They are murky brown and far too large for his face, making him appear insect-like and, due his receding hairline, far older than he is. His thin lips and small but flared nostrils collaborate to reinforce the impression. He possesses a remarkably expressive face, like silly putty, moist and red from the effort of maintaining the pose. Able to manipulate his features with startling ease, Joseph exploits his talent for all it is worth. 'Some people are here for a reason,' he muses. 'They can do something better than anyone else, something extraordinary.' Joseph believes he is one of those people. He has been chosen.

The candle flames dance across his face and flicker in his eyes, filling him with mischief. He glows the way he imagines a famous painting might glow as people marvelled at it. He dangles like an obscene party decoration, swaying like a broken chandelier with a celebrity smile.

Joseph croons his birthday song in a wavering baritone. 'Happy birrrrthdayyy, King Joseph… Happy birthday to meeeeee…' he sings.

He pauses for effect and then slowly bows his head, signalling to the audience that his performance is at an end. Rapturous applause rings in his ears and Joseph basks in the spotlight. Unfortunately, the applause he hears is oddly animated and overly familiar. It is canned and mechanical, rewarding his tenacity, his ingenuity, with pre-recorded praise. And Joseph wants more, much more. Somewhere, he ponders, there is a sign that lights up when I smile, when I think of something clever, it flashes in purple neon, Applause! Applause! Applause!

Regrettably, not everything is going according to his master plan. Joseph's grasp on the fan is tenuous and complicated by the unnatural arch of his back. To make matters worse, an itch on his inner thigh has gone unscratched, and others are forming, nibbling on his neck and chest. He yearns to free one of his arms and tend to the itches, but Joseph knows if he does that, he will risk falling from the fan. And if he falls now, before his guests arrive, his birthday will be ruined. The look on their faces as they each walk through the door will be worth it, he thinks.

King Joseph, Lord of all Birthdays.

King Joseph, Master of Surprise.

Joseph surveys his kingdom from above and is momentarily dismayed by its stillness, the way it defines him, calling upon him to fill its emptiness. Still, it will soon be crowded with his loyal subjects, and Joseph can hardly wait. He is, however, concerned about his crown. It is tilting dangerously close to one side of his head and is torn and wet with perspiration. Hold on just a little while longer, he thinks, just a few more minutes, and the show will begin.

Each guest received a personal summons, but not via the post or the telephone. No. They know who they are, instinctively, intuitively. It is a surprise party after all. Joseph has neither mentioned it, nor extended so much as a hint that he knows what they are up to. But he does, oh yes, he knows what they have planned.

King Joseph, Clairvoyant.

King Joseph, Soothsayer.

Suddenly, Joseph has the most curious feeling, as if he is being watched. He turns his head and notices the ceiling fan Switch on the far wall. It is a rectangular plastic box, emblazoned with silver numbers that encircle a mouth-like dial. Something about it distresses him. He gets the distinct impression that it is leering at him. Is it conspiring to ruin his party before it has even begun?

Gripped by a terrible foreboding, he begins to panic. If the Switch were to wish it, he thinks, it could trigger the fan. After all, that is its power, its purpose. It could, if it so desired, send him tumbling from the sky. It could ruin everything. Joseph nervously bites his bottom lip. He narrows his big brown eyes at the Switch, evaluating it, trying to ascertain the extent of the threat.

Torn between excitement, dread, and nervous agitation, Joseph considers his options. Perhaps, if he befriends the Switch, it won't interfere? He senses that winning it over will not be easy. After all, he did not invite it to the party and it must feel a little miffed about that. Joseph experiences a spasm of guilt. Perhaps he has judged it too swiftly? It must at least have expected the courtesy of an acknowledgement, a neighbourly hello.

Joseph smiles at the Switch, raising his eyebrows and conveying polite remorse with his eyes. 'Sorry,' he attempts to say with the expression, 'I am afraid I am guilty of neglect.'

'That is quite all right, your highness,' he expects the Switch to say in turn, 'for I am just honoured to be here.'

Yet the Switch says nothing. Joseph waits for a forgiving smile in return, but the Switch is obviously not buying it. It has clearly run out of patience and is now beyond any effort he might make to console it. Great, he thinks, all I need is a Switch with a grudge; a disgruntled gatecrasher on a revenge trip. Joseph feels sick with dread. It's going to spoil everything, he thinks, and all it needs to do is activate the fan.

Joseph is suddenly struck by an idea. Perhaps if I entertain the Switch, he thinks, if I give it a private show, a peek at the big event, it might forgive me? Perhaps if I woo it, charm it a little bit, it might even give a little speech at the party? That would be marvellous, he thinks. He imagines how impressed his guests will be.

'This is my friend, the ceiling fan Switch,' he will gush to those gathered, 'and we've been through a lot together.'

Joseph steadies himself and clears his throat. He takes a few deep breaths and waits for the applause to die down. When it is quiet, he begins to sing, feeling it, crooning with renewed passion and striving to make each note grander and more sweeping than the last. He dazzles the Switch with his smile, flashing his teeth and fluttering his eyelashes as he bellows the words. But after a few minutes of throwing himself into the performance, Joseph's voice grows coarse and his throat begins to sting. He begins to fret all over again, sensing that the Switch is unimpressed. His back and arms ache from the strain of holding onto the fan. They are not going to get here in time, he thinks. Deflated and ashamed, he looks down upon his lavish party feast. Those candles will not last forever, he thinks. The flames are hovering dangerously low, lingering above the layers of fresh cream, jam and sponge. Echoing through the trickles of smoke, the same thought returns to Joseph: what if I fall from the sky?

He focuses on remaining calm, blocking out all but the persistent throb of his pulse and the hungry ebb of his breaths. He listens intently, and to his horror he soon hears a voice. It is the Switch. It must be.

'I shall put out those flames, Joseph. Yes, I will. With just a fleeting twitch, I will murder the small dancing fires.'

'You will do no such thing,' Joseph blurts back.

'Is that so?' says the Switch.

'Yeah…it yeah it is,' Joseph stammers nervously.

'What are you going to do to stop me, Birthday Boy?'

'I'll tell everyone you're a party pooper. Nobody likes a party pooper.'

'Be my guest.'

'What?'

'I said, Be. My. Guest.'

'I'm not anybody's guest and neither are you. I didn't invite you and now you're upset, admit it!'

'I couldn't care less,' the Switch scoffs, and then adds, 'They're not coming, you know.'

'Yes, they are! And I'm going to tell them all about what you are and what you've done,' he says.

'What am I, Joseph?'

'You're a fucking wall fixture, a bitter, lonely, uninvited Switch!'

'What have I done?'

'You're trying to ruin the party.'

'Who are you going to tell?'

'Them…' Joseph replies boldly.

'Who?' the Switch asks again.

Joseph's eyes dart around the room, searching in vain for someone to corroborate his story. But his guests have not yet arrived, and the invisible audience jeers at him. He exerts every ounce of his will to resist the tears that are filling his eyes. He snaps at the air with his teeth and his tongue writhes across his lips, lapping at invisible sores. A small trickle of drool slowly gathers on the tip of his chin. It balances like sweet icing on his birthday face.

'Gatecrasher!' he sobs dramatically. 'Gatecrashergatecrashergate crashergate…'

The Switch is suddenly silent, and raucous laughter explodes from Joseph's throat.

'Pussy cat got your tongue?' Joseph roars. 'Fucking Party Pooper!'

Joseph stretches his words with clever abandon. He fills his cheeks with air to appear bigger than he is.

'Listen carefully, Birthday Boy!' the Switch hisses, suddenly cutting Joseph's gleeful tirade short. 'It'is time I murdered the fires…the small dancing fires,' it says, 'for where are your party guests? And how firm is your birthday grip? For soon you will surely slip, and the echoes of my laughter will ring out, long after your birthday is dead.'

Joseph suddenly feels his hands slip from the steel spine of the fan, and he frantically scrambles to regain his grip. He farts loudly, wetly, and a high-pitched girly squeal escapes his lips. To his dismay, the small bead of drool that had gathered on his chin suddenly leaves him, and helplessly, he watches it fall towards his birthday cake. 'Noooooo!' he gasps in horror.

The Switch erupts into a fit of frothing laughter. Joseph winces as escalating spasms of hysteria fill the small white room. His precious drool envelopes one of the burning candles and instantly snuffs it out. A tiny explosion of funeral pyre smoke spirals upwards.

Joseph turns his face, aglow with the vengeful flicker of the surviving flames, to rest upon the murderous Switch. He farts again, this time deliberately, and his pasty white buttocks quiver from the trumpeted spluttering of his rancorous sphincter. An eloquent, poetic stench fills his flared nostrils and the fan quakes and trembles above him. There had been twenty-one candles alight and now there are only twenty.

Hot tears well in his eyes and blur his vision. 'Where are you? Reveal yourself!' he panics.

'I am where I have always been, Joseph,' the Switch replies.

'Where is that?'

'Have a guess…'

Joseph's mind reels with deplorable possibilities. Wildly shaking his head from side to side and blinking, his eyes begin to clear. Yet he still cannot locate the Switch.

'I'll give you a clue,' the voice ventures, and then, 'Mmmmm… this tastes really good! Did your Mummy make it for you?'

'You leave my Mummy out of it!' Joseph snaps.

'Do you think Mummy would bake a cake just for me?'

'No! No! No! Never ever-ever-ever!'

'Oh, I think she might, Joseph.'

Joseph is speechless. An image of the Switch crawling towards his birthday cake like a hungry mechanical spider fills his mind. That little fucker is mobile, the bastard's got legs, he thinks. Joseph imagines the plastic monstrosity humping his birthday cake, like a dog on someone's leg, greedily swallowing chunks of sponge, jam and fresh cream.

'Mmmmm… Thank you so much, Mummy… Mmmm…this is delicious!' slobbers the Switch.

'You…you…you better not be eating my cake!' Joseph stammers in outrage.

Joseph sharply twists his head so that he can see the cake directly beneath him, and his eyes finally clear. The birthday cake is untouched and the remaining candles still burn brightly. Joseph is relieved, but he feels a little silly. He decides he was being paranoid and is about to tell the Switch off, to give it a piece of his mind, when he feels the tissue-paper crown slip from his head and fall towards the cake.

'Oh noooo!'

'Oh yesssssssss…' the Switch hisses.

Joseph watches in terror as the paper crown wafts from one side of the room to the other, gently falling towards his precious birthday cake. The crown dips and twirls, surfing on ghostly air currents. Just as it appears it will land safely beside the cake, it suddenly turns. With a final nudge of encouragement from the Switch and a lithe breath of plastic air, it settles squarely on the burning candles and instantly catches ablaze. Smoke billows into the room in thick torrents. The explosion of fire is so instant and bright and the smoke so nauseating that Joseph feels like he might be sick. In a few moments, it is all over and the cake's cream top is covered in black ash. A few renegade embers circle the room like flies over a caramelised carcass.

'If you are a king, then where is your crown?' the Switch jibes.

Joseph feels like letting go of the fan and barricading the door so that nobody will see what he has become. The king has relinquished his crown. He is a peasant, a common fool and nothing more. For who will love him now?

But wait, he thinks, what of the candles? Joseph looks downward. His candles are still ablaze. To his astonishment, the very same candle he extinguished with his drool is once again alight. His fallen crown reignited it.

King Joseph, Worker of Miracles.

King Joseph, Birthday Messiah.

Twenty-one. He beams with pride; it is my birthday and I am twenty-one. King Joseph feels invigorated, exonerated. His hands tear at the fan's slippery spine, shaking it violently, viciously. The sharp crackle of plaster and paint fills the room as fragments of ceiling skin fall into birthday oblivion. With each metal groan, a particle of Joseph's triumph is reborn. Not once does he take his eyes off the ominous Switch. The fan drops a few inches, and the small section of ceiling that holds it in place splinters and showers Joseph in white dust. He sharply inhales, coughing and spluttering as the particles of paint and plaster quickly overwhelm his lungs. The fan buckles, unhinging further, reacting to his swaying weight and the force of his convulsions. He readies himself for the fall.

Joseph jerks the fan from side to side, willing it to liberate itself, to fall with him from the sky. With a last unholy thrust, the fan finally breaks, disconnecting from the ceiling. A sudden flood of intestinal wiring erupts from the hole and shatters Joseph's grip. They fall together from the wound, plummeting towards the cake on the floor; Joseph and the ceiling fan above him, plummeting together as if in slow motion. He twists his body and dexterously flips over in the air, extending into a graceful swan dive. Joseph thrusts his arms behind himself like wings and points his toes back at the hole in the sky. Halfway between the ceiling and the floor, in the space between worlds, Joseph fixes careful aim upon his birthday cake. Sucking breath into his lungs until he feels they might burst, Joseph finally unleashes a powerful gush of air from his cheeks. In one glorious swoop he completely extinguishes his birthday candles, snuffing out the ceremonial fires with one mighty birthday breath.

Joseph would like to smile, to freeze time and marvel at what he has accomplished. Instead, his face collides with the blackened cake.

Impact.

There is no time to make a wish and nobody to celebrate his glorious descent. Joseph's face crushes the cake in an explosion of cream, jam and sponge. Multicoloured jelly beans and chocolate bullet shrapnel whizz through the air like buckshot. The fan follows closely behind, slamming into the back of Joseph's skull like an impossible birthday kiss.

And then the blood…

Blood staining the whites of his eyes…

Blood painting their strange embrace…

Joseph groans in satisfied agony. His face writhes in the demolished cake and he turns and peels off the sweets that have stuck to his face, leaving colourful indentations in his skin. The back of his head aches terribly and he wonders if the fan has left a hole there, an escape route for his thoughts. Choking back the thick, salty fluid that is rapidly filling his mouth, he struggles to rise but finds that he cannot. He whimpers feebly, squirming like a worm in the sweet gore. Summoning the last vestiges of his will, he finally manages to roll over onto his back. A wave of sickness envelopes him and he segues into darkness.

He awakens some time later to find himself lying on his back on the floor. He shakes his head and globules of snot and dark red drool whip from his face and freckle the walls. Straining desperately to regain his vision, Joseph blinks and snorts out the deposits of sponge cake clogging his nostrils.

In the furthest corner of his eye, Joseph discovers a small, clear white space. Curiously, he peers through it. There on the wall of his room he sees the Switch: defeated, vanquished by love. A large dollop of ashen cream and his own blood trickles from its dial like drool. He lifts his head, wanting to be certain that the murderous Switch can see the expression on his face.

When he is certain that it can see deep into his eyes, the corners of Joseph's mouth twist into a triumphant grin. 'Happy birthday, King Joseph,' he says. 'Happy birthday to me...'

Now lying on his side, he allows his head to rest in the entrails of the demolished cake and closes his eyes.

Moments later, the door to the room swings open and a woman appears. She has a cake under her arm. The outside light frames her willowy limbs, her white pulled-back hair and frail posture. Her pale grey eyes briefly scan the mess on the floor and walls. Her disapproval and annoyance are familiar to Joseph, who has opened one eye and is looking vacantly in her direction.

'Well, you've done it again, haven't you, Joseph?' she says irritably. 'How many times do I have to clean up your mess before you learn? Have you ever considered that it might be a good idea to eat your birthday cake instead of painting the walls with it?'

Yet when she looks down at Joseph on the floor, scanning his face for signs of remorse, the worried crease in her brow disappears. She smiles at him fondly and kneels at his side, putting the new cake next to the scattered remains of the one she brought in yesterday. She fusses over him, wiping cream and jam from under his eye and from the corners of his mouth with a lace handkerchief.

'It's really stuffy in here, Joseph,' she says suddenly. 'Have you been playing with the air conditioner switch again?'

Joseph does not reply.

The hole in the sky and the fallen ceiling fan are nowhere to be seen.

Gladys Slattery stands up and strides purposely over to the switch on the wall. It is covered in what looks like blood. Alarmed, she runs her finger across the switch and puts some of the sticky red substance on her tongue to taste it. She realises immediately that it is just jam from the cake, but she just wanted to be sure. She slowly twists the dial to the right and pauses as the hum of the air conditioner spills from the vents in the ceiling and begins cooling the padded cell.

She turns and looks at her son lying on the floor. His eyes are blank and formless, they betray nothing, seem to reflect nothing. She watches him sadly, her heart aching. She walks out of the room, hoping to procure some cleaning materials to fix up the mess. She leaves the newly baked birthday cake, still covered in cling wrap, next to her son.

Joseph, now alone again, continues to stare from his place on the floor into the ceiling sky. It is as if he is searching for something important that he has lost or misplaced, and any moment it will return to him.

Then again, perhaps he is yearning for something that was never there to begin with.

Carl

'What's your name?'

'Ant.'

'Wow, yeah, I'm Ant too. Who'd have thunk it?'

'I think you'll find it's a really common name around here.'

'Yeah? You seem smart. Are you an, um, an interloper...?'

'You mean an intellectual.'

'Yes, that's it! I thought there was something different about you.'

'I'm not that different, Ant, just been here a while longer than you, I suspect.'

'Yeah? It feels like ages since we've been marching like this. In, um...in...'

'In formation?'

'Yep, I guess that's what this is: Information. Do you ever get tired?'

'No.'

'Jesus, I'm knackered, Ant. I really could do with a break. Do we get those?'

'No, we don't. Who is Jesus?'

'Huh?'

'Jesus...you just said Jesus. Who or what is that?'

'Dunno, dude. The word just popped into my head. Do you know the ones marching ahead of us?'

'Everyone here is called Ant. I'm called Ant. You're called Ant. Ant is all.'

'Oh yeah? Ant is all, huh? Sounds kind of cosmic.'

'It is. You're not as dumb as you appear. Except...well, I don't know if I should say...'

'No, go on. You were going to tell me something.'

'Well, about five Ants in front of you there's a fellow named Carl.'

'No way! Carl! Far out! Do you know him personally?'

'Not really.'

'Christ! I'd do anything to meet him.'

'What?'

'I said I'd like to know this Carl dude.'

'No, before that. You said a word – Christ?'

'Oh yeah, Christ. This is getting embarrassing. Look, I'll level with you, Ant. I heard the Monster say it a bunch of times. It stuck in my head.'

'The Monster? Who is this monster you speak of?'

'You haven't seen the Monster?'

'No.'

'All you have to do is look up. Look up here and there and you'll see the Monster. It has the biggest, most curious eyes you ever saw. The Monster likes to watch us march.'

'Ant doesn't look up. Ant is all.'

'Yeah well, the Monster is up there in the sky if you look and it talks. I once heard it say those very words right before it reached down and squished some dude. It was horrifying. Snuffed him out and then said "Jesus Christ!" – cursing like. The Monster has a huge white pointing thing that he squishes dudes with, like… um…a finger? Is that even a word – finger?'

'No, that isn't a word or a thing. You just made it up. What is wrong with you? Are you insane?'

'To be honest, I'm not really certain, Ant. I bet Carl would know though. Should I ask him?'

'Suit yourself, Ant. But I don't like your chances.'

'Why is that?'

'You need to stay in formation, at least until we get to… Oh, never mind…'

'No wait! Get to where exactly? Where are we going?'

'I am not at liberty to say.'

'God, you're a secretive bastard, Ant. Where are we marching to?'

'Okay. It's called Calvary. But if anyone asks, I didn't tell you that.'

'Calvary? Don't you mean Colostomy?

'I know what I said, Ant. Don't be so disagreeable.'

'Sorry. I'm busting for a toilet break and running out of options. Please go on.'

'We march to Calvary and then we disappear into the black hole we dug on top and it gets really, really dark and then if you're lucky they give you special orders.'

'What then?'

'Then we get to go on special missions.'

'Sounds like fun. What constitutes a special mission? Wait, did I just say constitutes?'

'Yes, you did and no, Ant, once again it isn't a word.'

'Sorry, I can't even claim I got that one from the Monsters.'

'What? There's more than one Monster?'

'I suspect so. Why? Does that scare you?'

'It makes me feel a little uneasy, yes. All this talk of the finger and the Jesus and the Monster would freak out any sane Ant. I suspect that you're a fearmonger. You get off on scaring the willies out of anyone naïve enough to listen to your nonsensical babble. I'm an intellectual, as you so rightly observed. I can see right through your games. I suggest you keep your eyes forward and not talk about this stuff to anyone. You could get in a lot of trouble.'

'Man, you really are a stuffy bastard. I bet Carl isn't so stuck-up and narrow-minded. I'm going to see if I can go on a special mission with Carl. You know, just hang out, shoot the shit, like bros. He at least sounds interesting.'

'That's perfectly fine with me.'

'Fine! I will then. You'll see.'

'Fine!!'

'Fine!!!'

'Fine!!!!'

'Hey, I can see Carl from here! Hey, Carl! Hey, dude! Back here! Hmmm, he appears to be occupied. Wait, he's carrying something, it looks heavy. That's Carl, isn't it? The dude carrying the…the thing?'

'It's called a cross.'

'Why is Carl carrying a cross?'

'They're going to nail him to it when we get to Calvary.'

'Really? That's horrible. What did Carl do to deserve that?'

'Basically, Carl is a smart arse. He's completely insane, much like you, Ant. He insisted he was different, special, thus the name Carl. He reckoned we should drop everything: giant breadcrumbs, delicious curried chickpea chunks, all of the stuff that falls from the sky just for us – drop it all and follow him.'

'But we are following him.'

'Yeah, I suppose you got that part right. You know how you called me an intellectual?'

'Yes.'

'Well, that is what I like to call irony. Unlike the Jesus and the finger, it is an actual thing, Ant. Carl is an arrogant little shit-stirrer with delusions of grandeur. Ant is all. Carl is going to get what he deserves.'

'But I thought we were on our way to the big dark hole and then we were going on special missions. Jesus Christ Finger, this is too much, Ant! I have to warn Carl.'

'I wouldn't do that if I were you.'

'Carl! Hey, Carl! Look out, dude…they're gonna nail you to that thing!'

'Don't be an idiot, Ant. Keep your eyes forward, your mouth shut and stay in formation.'

'Hey, Carl is making a break for it. He's broken ranks, dropped the cross. Go, Carl! Run like the wind, you mad bastard!'

'Shut up, you fool!'

'Hey! Look up! Now, Ant! Look up and you'll see…it's the Monster!'

'No, it isn't.'

'Yes, it is. Hey, Monster! Heyyyyyy! We're down here!'

'There is no Monster.'

'O-oh, shit…now he's done it. Jesus bloody Christ… Here comes that damn finger again! It's going after Carl! No! Nooo! Nooooooo!'

*

'I don't think Carl is gonna make it, dude… He looks pretty fucked-up.'

'Just keep marching, Ant. Keep your eyes forward, stay in formation and just march…'

The Donkey and the Pigeon

(A Love Story)

Whenever 'the Donkey' arrived on set, reeking of expensive cologne and stale cum, his presence was met with a respectful silence. Hushed whispers and salacious gossip from his circle of admirers and co-workers was inevitable. Every time Noah Fargone dropped his pants, there was the same reaction: an awestruck inhalation of collective breath. For obvious reasons, Noah had adopted the term 'the Donkey' when he first began dabbling in the profession. Although preferring the fairer sex in his regular life, he indulged in a wide array of sexes, sizes and genders on camera; the money was simply too good to turn down.

The Donkey didn't bat for the pink team, but he fucked them all, and a plethora of nubile babes to boot, like an aroused zombie on a rotating flesh carousel. He was more concerned with the pay cheque, the glory of the rolling cameras and his rising online fame, than anything authentically satisfying. His extraordinarily shaped and bent member, when fully erect, would elicit gasps of wonderment from the most stoic of onlookers and the introverted perverts who gathered around him, secretly lusting for the Donkey's attention, like moths drawn to an engorged purple flame.

If you were on the receiving end of Noah Fargone's expertise, your trumpeted flatulence, once cheery and musical, would soon devolve into a spluttering and breathy series of confused question marks and eventually, complete and utter silence. One's farts would dither into insignificance, like Picasso's bruised, blue-period arsehole, never to be heard from again.

The Donkey was a star. At least, Caroline thought so; she held the boom microphone for most of his filmed fuck sessions. He had a thousand-yard stare, thought Caroline, like a half-baked Steve McQueen, with a cock so ridiculously big that in any industry or reality other than this one, it would be an enormous inconvenience. Caroline's head would jabber forwards and backwards as she held the boom mic, like an epileptic pigeon that was desperately attempting to appear professional. In truth, she was simply enraptured by the Donkey's artful buggerings. She couldn't help but quiver, Caroline, her head a seesawing light bulb of nervousness and awe. And Noah studied her, duly noting this about her character, marvelling at her petite but crookedly carved Jewish nose. Her luminous and determined hazel eyes beheld pupils that defined her as student and servant, dilating in the manner of an admirer of narcissists and deviants. Her small breasts, nipples pert and confused, heaved with heavy breaths beneath her sweat-soaked white T-shirt.

'Fetch me a bottle of Avian water, Pigeon,' Noah often said to her between fuck scenes. It was a callous but flirtatious power move that delighted Noah, and endlessly frustrated Caroline. Although she studied the Donkey with admiration, for his reckless sexual prowess and moral ambiguity, she was nonetheless perturbed by his arrogant disposition.

In time, Caroline reluctantly accepted that she was the carrier Pigeon; the deliverer of Viagra pills, top-shelf vodka and hand-held mirrors streaked with lines of primo cocaine. Noah Fargone, the Donkey of her dreams, was also the irascible rooster of her favourite nightmares; a cock worth running errands for.

So, when Noah Fargone took his own life at the age of twenty-four, it was a surprise to everyone but Caroline.

The Pigeon had seen him up close for hundreds of hours, fucking away his pain. To everyone else in the industry, the Donkey had seemed to have it all. He was one of the most watched and celebrated porn stars in Moralpanik. His films, both debauched and punishingly erotic, were viewed by millions of like-minded perverts throughout the city. Caroline had stared deep into his cold blue eyes and she knew exactly why he topped himself: rejection.

Every time Noah Fargone had propositioned her, she had turned him down. Despite her obvious obsession with the man, she just wasn't willing to give him what he wanted. It would have tarnished her self-respect, which was already diminished due to his infantile demands and the insistency of his advances. It had become almost pathetic.

The Donkey would never get to fuck his Pigeon. The Donkey was alone, and no amount of money or drugs or smutty fame would change that. But the Pigeon listened. The Pigeon seemed to care. The Pigeon had been moved to tears as he recalled the childhood of extreme sexual abuse and violence that precluded his successful career, forever distorting his journey into manhood. The Pigeon loved him. No one else did, not really. She loved his enormous member and his pain-filled heart. The Pigeon loved the real Donkey. Yet the Pigeon was the only bird in the aviary that refused to fuck him. Why? And off camera too, which made it all the worse. The Pigeon said no, no, no, and the Donkey, distressed by rejection and unaccustomed to such resilience, took a fatal overdose of painkillers and Champaign in his condo and died alone.

At Noah Fargone's funeral, all the industry heavy weights were there. Silicone tits and their numb nipples stood at attention. Shiny leather gays with hairy backs crept creepily and in full view. Red vinyl thigh-high boots and stilettos glimmered, desperate to be admired. Butt-plug victims swayed uneasily on their feet, thinking only of themselves and their loosening plight. Wannabe shaved-pussy, catwalk monsters pretended to weep and inevitably failed. Anally bleached blondes and brunettes with drug-fucked eyes did nothing to hide what was flowing through their veins and blood, walking like they'd ridden too many magical unicorns too many times. Directors with cheap seventies moustaches mused on the event and thought instead about going home to their mansions and doing more blow.

And then there was Caroline. Yes, Caroline, who sauntered up to the open coffin at his funeral with determination and a plan. When it seemed to her that everyone had viewed the body for the last time, she made her move. And, after sadly searching Noah Fargone's lifeless face for signs of true beauty, depth or remorse, in which case she found none, Caroline stealthily retrieved a small but very sharp knife from her jacket. The Pigeon unzipped the Donkey's pants and, bending over the coffin and holding his immense but flaccid member in her firm grip, she sliced off his penis at the root and quickly slotted it into her open handbag. At first, nobody seemed to notice. As she casually walked from the room, she heard the unmistakable murmurings of the gathered throng. She noticed that the winking eye of Noah Fargone's severed penis was peeking out of the top of her handbag.

'You did good, Pigeon,' it seemed to say.

In life, as in death, thought Caroline, the Donkey's cock was just too big to comfortably fit into anything.

As the hysteria and shock in the funeral parlour reached a climax, Caroline turned to view the open coffin one more time before she left, just to see what had everyone so startled. A small fountain of iridescent blood pissed enthusiastically from the wooden box, and from Noah's vandalised crotch, like a pitiful but determined garden sprinkler.

Caroline smiled. She tightly gripped Noah Fargone's protruding member in her bag and was surprised to notice that it seemed to have gotten harder. Rock-hard, in fact. Caroline, ignoring the background screams of horror, then whipped the Donkey's massive, stiffening cock out of her handbag and twirled it above her head like the blades of a retarded helicopter. When she reached the kerb – filled with a renewed sense of adventure and regaled by the whisperings of Noah Fargone's impossible love – she proceeded to try to hail a taxicab with his severed dick.

After a few minutes of macabre baton twirling, Caroline was almost ready to give up. Spotting a taxicab approaching from the opposite direction, she edged ever closer to the middle of the road to hail it down. The Pigeon was hit at top speed by a yellow school bus filled with children. She died instantly. The light in her eyes was snuffed out, like a candle flame pinched between wet, pornographic fingers.

The bus screeched to a halt. The Donkey's rock-hard penis soared through the air and connected with the vehicle's windscreen, so erect that the impact cracked the glass. It sat there for a few moments, just hanging on, like a giant alien slug. Then it slid downward, almost as if in slow motion, and the bus driver's mouth gaped open in shock. It was the biggest goddamn todger she had ever seen.

The children, bewildered by the sudden impact, stared in terror at the Donkey's immense penis as it slithered from the fractured glass. Leaving a trail of blood and cum and broken dreams, Noah Fargone's only redeeming feature descended, halting when it connected with a bent windscreen wiper and stalling, becoming wedged there. Without knowing how to react, what to think, or what to do or feel, the children did the most appropriate thing possible under the circumstances: they all began to scream.

The Scribe

When I first awoke from the dream, it was very, very dark. In fact, it was so dark that for a moment I could not fathom where I was. Then I saw a tiny bead of piercing light in the distance. I walked towards it. Determined to re-enter the outside world, I crawled out of a clammy black hole – no bigger than a pinprick – in the back of my own head. I fell several badly written stories, spiralling like a concrete feather, ploughing into the surface of an undiscovered planet. I found myself, instead, cowering beneath the sweat soaked sheets of my bed. I sat bolt upright. My eyes steadily adjusted to my surroundings. They were filled with crusty yellow jots of sleep gunk, and I wearily wiped them away.

The dream had inspired a sense of purpose in me, although the details were sketchy at best. Without truly knowing why, I was now resolute; I would reinvent myself as a Grand Scribe, as a writer of rippling fictions and cheerful tragedy. Steeling my resolve, I leapt out of bed and wandered into the lounge room. I proceeded to look around me for inspiration.

Curled up in a ball on the mat, just inside the front door of my house, was my neighbour's cat. A particularly scruffy and weather-beaten animal, gunmetal-grey with a white patch over one eye. He always seemed to be hanging around my place during the week when his owner was at work. Although I didn't even know his name, I nevertheless encouraged his vagrancy with the occasional bowl of milk and an affectionate stroke. I left the kitchen window slightly ajar so he could come and leave as he pleased.

It occurred to me that the image I beheld was of two possible protagonists, the Mat and the Cat. They could provide the creative fuel for an interesting yet simple story. I had never really written much in the past and I had to start somewhere. So I decided to write something down and seek out random people and see what they thought.

I started with 'The Cat sat on the Mat.'

I went out into the street, clearly elated by my first attempt at writing. Puffing out my chest and gathering all my bravado, I started crowing to the passers-by, rather loudly, exactly what I had written. There was little response.

After a long while, an old lady, clearly disturbed yet also kind, said, 'That's nice, dear,' and proceeded to scurry away.

I chased her down the street, egged on by my only feedback of the day. Repeating my mantra in desperate tones, hoping for some further critical appraisal. She batted me down with her handbag and uttered something about calling the police.

I stormed home, stepping over the Cat on the Mat so as not to disturb their strange symbiotic embrace. Once inside, I threw myself onto the couch and groaned in anguish. So this is what they call existential angst, I thought. Being a writer certainly came with some serious pitfalls. Had I really thought this whole writer business through? Why had my writing outraged the old lady so? Was it unoriginal? Perhaps I needed a new angle? A writer needs readers, I thought, so I will attempt to have my writing actually read. Ha! Yes, that will be the proof that I am well on my way.

Yet my first draft continued to daunt me. I needed a twist, something people would not expect. I wanted to shock, interest and beguile. I wanted to send my readers a deliberate yet dazzling display of what I was truly capable of.

I wrote, 'The Mat sat on the Cat and the Cat spat!'

I was finally getting somewhere. All I needed now was a reader. So, I took the piece of paper with said masterpiece scrawled upon it to the local bus stop. I placed it on the seat and stood some metres away, just out of eyeshot, and waited for the first reader to arrive. I waited for some time. Eventually a guy in a cowboy hat and acid-wash jeans sat down just inches away from my magnum opus. At first, he paid no attention to the piece of paper at his side, but then he glanced at it for a moment. He winced at what I imagined was an attempt at reading and then looked away. No sooner had I found my first reader than a bus arrived and he got on it and cruised away. Incensed, I chased after the bus. I waved my manuscript in the air and hollered that he was not only inconsiderate, but possibly illiterate.

Throughout the next three hours the same situation recurred with unnerving regularity. I eventually concluded that my writing was not yet good enough for public consumption. Besides, running after all those buses was tiring. I was exhausted and my throat was coarse from the incessant yelling.

The Cat spat? Who wants to read about an angry Cat, and the personification of an arrogant and possibly murderous Mat?

Then I realised the obvious: everyone does.

Who was this miserable Mat anyway? What made it hate the feline species so? Was this Cat so despicable that a Mat would surely despise and hate him so? Can such discomfort – being sat upon and spat at and riddled with flea-infested fur – prompt murderous revenge from a Mat who never meant any harm to anyone?

At this point, I thought, the sensible thing would be for the Mat to write me a letter. It would be a subtle plea on its part, something to get my attention. And after all, the personal touch always seems to work. A letter would help it to air its grievances, to make its feelings crystal clear.

Instead, I received this:

Petty Human, hearken to me!

Wipe your soles upon me, smear me with your dirty boots and muddied ways so that I might cleanse your hell-bound soles. For that is my role, it is the point of my existence. But I warn you, do not let that Cat sit upon me a moment longer. He cares not for my rubber lining, nor does he respect the bristling of my surface face.

Let him be damned or put out to pasture; to piss and leave his vile scent upon your garden beds and trees instead of me. Spare me from this despicably lazy feline, for I itch uncontrollably and cannot move. I am so infested with parasites and irritated by his preternatural warmth that I can barely breathe.

This Cretin, your beloved pet, he digs his razor-sharp claws deep into my skin as if I had no discernible feelings at all. Clearly, he has no idea the danger he is in, as I meticulously plot each murderous step of my revenge. Human, you too will feel my scourge when your carpets are diseased and dirty and your clawed slave is dead, dead, dead.

Yours in anguish, Mat.

Unfortunately, I found the letter to be petulant and unnecessarily indignant. Who did this Mat think it was? Still, I conceded, at least now there was a motive. A potential murderer and escapee took form on the pages in my mind. But was it enough for the bus stop? Indeed, was it enough to *stop* that bloody bus?

Oh, if only the bus were to suddenly grind to a halt and everyone aboard were to race from its doors and riot around me. Was it enough to be swamped with readers, in the middle of a street roaring with traffic, demanding to know what happens next?

I knew the answer before it had even formed as a question in my head. It was certainly not. A world sprawling with curious readers would need to howl out in distraught mayhem, as one, before I was satisfied that I was done. As it was, they would not rise and picket the streets, pleading with the governments of the globe to flatly demand the Mat's ultimate and triumphant emancipation.

'Let the Mat go!' they should rightly shout.

'Cast the Cat outside and let the Mat be a Door Mat in peace!'

It occurred to me then, that, unfortunately, I had told but a fraction of the story. I was tempted to take my expanding narrative to a larger venue, like a football or cricket game, to test its glory upon the people there. I could roam among the crowd and bellow it unto the masses. But I realised, quite wisely I thought, that I was perhaps being a tad hasty. My dilemma was one of creative craving and an almost unbearable impatience for cultural impact and change. Not to mention the longing for critical praise and the adoration that I imagine every great writer attains, at a certain point, for the obvious and complete mastery over their carefully honed craft.

I looked over at the Cat and wondered if he knew the danger he was in? These multiple worlds sprawling with reality and fiction could coexist in their current incarnation for only so long. What if something bad were to happen? Would I be to blame?

The Mat shifted seamlessly beneath the Cat. Its edges curled and flickered and its rubber corners strained to rise from the floor. Or did they? I felt too tired to focus on them any longer, and I decided to have a nap. Perhaps, once again, my dreams would inform the flow of creation and awaken me to new possibilities. So, I trudged into the bedroom and went to sleep.

At some unfathomable point I began to dream…

I dreamt of a world where everyone was a writer. It was a strange and startling place, where the clouds rained upwards and the trees grew down into the ground instead of up. Their roots, those most telling appendages, writhed above and around us all. This was the new world order, a desperate frontier mired in futility. People walked around with marker-pens and crayons poised in their hands, ready to write on everything and anything, even themselves. Others dragged typewriters through the streets at night and threw them through computer store windows to steal more efficient writing machines. Thoughts were written down as they were thought, dreams as soon as they could be remembered. On little notepads, people scrawled furiously, constantly, trying to keep up with their own minds so they could retain the keys to madness, genius and that fifty-fourth unpublished manuscript.

During my dream, and in this new world, I decided that I would be a writer no longer. For it was far more curious and backwards for someone to attempt to not be a writer. The few who did this, those who decided not to be, would be considered rebellious and subversive,

I thought. If one suddenly decided to work at not being a writer, one would actually be doing something. In my dream I was bucking trends. I was different. I was strangely appealing and unusually attractive to the writers that gathered, spellbound around me. I made the choice to not make choices, and so I refused to describe anything at all. I wrote nothing down.

In my dream, someone asked me what I did and I replied, 'I'm working at not being a writer.'

I was finally doing something with my life. I was undoing everything.

'Good for you, that's a good one,' people kept saying to me in the dream, 'but you know…you really should write that one down.'

When I awoke, I was face down in a puddle of my own dribble. I sensed changes, loss of time, hours hidden, days missing. I felt as if I had been writing in my sleep. My fingers ached and my mind raced with bizarre landscapes and distorted Cats and disgruntled Mats. I dragged myself into the kitchen and began to prepare a breakfast of toast, eggs and coffee. The jagged morning sun sliced through the partly open window, smearing light across my face and filling my eyes with an uninvited and oily glow. I peered out the window into the street, squinting as I loaded the toaster. A few of the neighbours had gathered on the footpath and were discussing something that appeared important. They pointed up and down the street, speaking to each other in urgent tones.

Another woman in a pink bathrobe and frayed slippers was calling out to what I assumed was her cat. 'Shifty! Heerrreee, Shifty!' she wailed.

Had something terrible occurred? I walked out to inspect the front Door Mat only to find that the Cat was no longer there. The Mat had a large tear in it and was half turned over. Tufts of cat fur scattered the carpet. No sooner had I stooped to further inspect the scene than there was a knock at the door. Nervously, I half opened it and peered outside.

A middle-aged man with a few strands of renegade hair plastered across his mostly balding scalp stood in the doorway. He seemed distraught. 'Have you seen my Pumpkin?' he asked.

'Um… What?' I replied.

'My Pumpkin, my Pumpkin…' he stammered. 'Have you seen my Pumpkin…my cat Pumpkin?'

'Oh…your cat! No, I don't think I have. Why? Has something happened?' I asked.

'All the cats in the neighbourhood seem to have gone missing. We've been calling for them and looking everywhere. We're all very worried, as you can imagine and…I was just wondering if you had seen or heard anything.'

Before I could muster an answer, I suddenly felt something brush against my leg, something rough and coarse that was probably *not a cat*! I began to panic as the reality of the situation sank in. I strained to look confused and concerned all at once, smiling at the man and discretely trying to kick aside the offending creature at the same time. I could not afford to let on that anything was amiss, not until I had investigated the situation for myself.

'No, I'm afraid I haven't seen your cat,' I said, 'but I will let you know first thing if I do. I don't keep pets, you see… Allergic to fleas, I'm afraid.' I scratched irritably at my neck for effect, and then, realising my blunder (itching would arouse suspicion rather than act as a clever ploy for sympathy,) I bade the man a good day and hastily closed the door in his face.

I stood there facing the inside of the door for some time, motionless, afraid to move. Behind me on the floor, I could almost hear the Mat thinking.

'You brought this on yourself,' it said. 'Now there is no limit to what I can do. Thank you, petty human, for through your inaction you have unknowingly unleashed me upon the world and my wrath shall be legendary in the annals of history. My Door Mat brethren will finally be free, freeeee, freeeeeeeeeee!'

It was quite a speech. Despite my reservations and mounting confusion, I felt myself swept away by the Mat's conviction. It was a rousing battle cry, one that could indeed inspire allegiance and act a catalyst for a Mat revolution, and perhaps even a war. I couldn't help but feel impressed.

Thinking carefully about this for a moment, I realised what I must do. I could not afford to be swayed by circumstantial sentiment and these dreams of grandiose vengeance. This Mat was clearly a charismatic despot in the making, a dangerously ambitious tyrant. Potentially, every house in every suburb in every city of the civilised world sheltered multiple versions of this rectangular fiend. The Cats of the world were in grave danger of extinction from an army of homicidal Door Mats. And their leader was right behind me. This Mat needed to be stopped before any more blood was shed, and it was up to me to do it. So without warning I turned and threw myself at the Mat.

Landing in a sprawling heap on the floor, mouth filled with tufts of fur, I looked up to see that I had slightly misjudged my attack. The Mat lay just out of my reach. I had either fallen way short or it had retreated just in time. Bruised and frustrated, I struggled to lift myself up onto my knees, keeping one eye on the Mat in case of any sudden tactical manoeuvres. Once I had my balance and my head had stopped spinning, I shuffled closer and prepared for the second wave of my offensive. The Mat lay deathly still, almost as if it were bleeding from the jagged rip in its centre. I paused for a second, inelegantly spluttering, spitting the fur from my lips and slurping a huge gulp of air into my lungs.

I launched myself at it once again, only this time I hit my target. Clenching the Mat's sides, I wrestled it from side to side, rolling about on the floor, over and over, viciously slamming it into the legs of the coffee table, endeavouring to tear at its wound further. After a few frenzied minutes, I realised the Mat was not resisting. It was just letting me fling it around. Without so much as a whimper, it had absorbed every one of my calculated blows. The Mat simply refused to fight back. I lay there looking up into the ceiling, the Mat limp at my side. I was exhausted, puzzled by this unexpected show of pacifistic resistance. It was as if the skinny spectacled ghost of Gandhi had appeared above us, and he was snickering at my futile display of violent action. This was no victory, I thought, it was a mortifying loss. Still, at least I had captured my foe. What now? Were the Mat and I to be encircled by one-way glass walls in a harshly lit interrogation chamber? Could I get a lengthy confession from this rogue rug? Somehow, I doubted it.

People needed to be warned about the impending pandemic, I decided. Who knows how many other Door Mats had been already infected by my own Mat's dangerous logic? Pet owners everywhere deserved to know this was happening. They needed to understand just how serious this threat was. It was a burden almost too heavy to bear, yet it was still my burden. Indeed, it was now my responsibility to break the bad news, to stem the uprising and bring about a new global awareness. I needed to get the word out.

But first I needed a forum, a way of reaching as many people as possible, and fast. Thinking back to my earlier internal monologue, I decided a packed sports arena would be my best shot. If I remembered correctly, there was a cricket game on at Moralpanik Stadium this very afternoon. It was a day–night match, so I figured I still had time. I needed to keep the newly pacified Mat close by, so I rolled it up and slid it firmly under one arm.

I caught the next bus and kept my head down. I couldn't afford to cause a panic, not yet. Looking around me at the other passengers, I realised just how fragile their realities were, how innocent and unaware. If only they knew what I knew. Very soon, their lives and the lives of their cats would be forever altered, changed irrevocably by the ever-shifting sands of time. As I stepped off the bus at my destination, I thanked the bus driver. It is funny how things change, I mused. Perhaps one day he will be thanking me. Yes, soon they will all be thanking me.

As I walked through the turnstiles and into Moralpanik Stadium, I felt nauseous, my stomach tied up in knots. I was a bundle of disconnected nerve endings, busily pulsing through the steps in my mind. It was as if I were about to begin my first official reading, I was that nervous.

I snuck into a seat at the back of the crowd so that I could survey the human landscape. The multi-hued crowd sprawled irregularly across the stands, some cheering, others merrily chatting amongst themselves. If I could get close enough to the edge of the field I would be within reach of my goal. Looking up, I noticed the game billboard, and it was immense, lit up with replays and advertisements. Slogans buzzed across its screen and hypnotised the multitude. I envisioned a picture of poor little Pumpkin emblazoned there, with the words, 'HAVE YOU SEEN THIS CAT?' flashing in bright neon. Swept away by infinite yet intangible sorrow, I felt the weight of the unconscious world bearing down heavily upon my shoulders.

I sprung into immediate action, stealthily slinking from seat to seat, ever closer to the barricade. Bobbing up and down, convulsing like a current of covert operative electricity. As I went, I decided to warm up the crowd, bit by bit. If I informed just a few of those gathered, I felt it might kick-start the message I needed to deliver. My warning would spread steadily through the gathered throng without drawing too much attention to me.

I sidled up to a man in a green and gold shirt with a thick layer of white zinc smeared across his nose. Tapping him on the arm to get his attention, I leaned in and whispered confidentially in his ear. 'The Mat sat on the Cat,' I said knowingly.

The man turned and looked at me blankly, slightly leaning away from me like I had just invaded his personal space.

I clearly repeated the information, 'The Mat sat on the Cat,' I stressed again.

Still, he didn't seem to understand the importance of my words. I crept away, moving on to my next target anyway. That's okay, I thought, he would soon.

I then slunk up to a married couple with two young children, speaking slightly louder this time so I would be heard I said, 'Your cat is in great danger.'

They too looked at me as if bewildered by the proposition, screwing up their faces as if I were mad.

'The Mat sat on the Cat,' I repeated, but it was to no avail.

Continuing along this path, I surged forward, zigzagging my way through the seething throng. One lady I frightened quite severely, sneaking up behind her and harshly hissing my mantra in her ear. She shrieked and threw her popcorn high into the air. It rained down upon us like a shower of buttered hailstones. My message would soon be rippling through this crowd, I mused. Vital information spreads like wildfire if disseminated wisely.

Once I had made my way to the barricade, I spied just what I was after: the team mascot. The scrawny carrot-top kid who wore the suit was sitting on the bench having a break. He'd taken off the huge fluffy lion's head from his outfit and laid it beside him. In a stroke of wild fortune, I noticed there was also a megaphone at his side.

Now I was ready to go. It was perfect timing, the players had just left the field for a drink break, so all the focus would be on me.

I leaned in to the red-headed kid. 'If you wanna go take a leak, I can keep an eye on these for you,' I said, pointing at the giant lion's head and megaphone.

The kid paused for a second, sizing me up. I could see he was seriously considering my offer. 'Um…yeah sure, thanks, man,' he replied. 'You sure you don't mind?'

'Not at all, bro,' I jived, warming to the kid's vibe.

As soon as he left, I promptly leapt the barricade and sat down in his place. My heart was beating like a jackhammer and I felt suddenly dizzy, reeling from the pressure I was under. Would I meet my own expectations? I would have my critics of course, I instinctively knew that. Still, it was essential I continued despite what a small rabble of cynical upstarts might think.

I slid the lion's head onto my shoulders and peered out through a slit just under the rubber mould of its inner face. It was a suffocating helm but a fitting disguise: the Lion, King of the Jungle and Lord of all Cats, Saviour of the Feline Race. I tried to breathe evenly, to stay calm. I was scared, I conceded, but wasn't that also a heroic trait?

I grabbed the megaphone and strode purposely, proudly, out into the middle of the pitch. From what I could see of the crowd, not many of them had noticed me yet. I arrived at a central point and turned on the megaphone. What am I going to say? Earlier on I felt I had the words right. I hadn't worried that I might choke or forget the correct way to swiftly deliver the warning. The megaphone suddenly squealed loudly and emitted a static-like buzz. People in the crowd started to murmur, there was a smattering of high-pitched laughter and a few jibes that I couldn't discern over the accumulated rumble of the slowly awakening thousands in the stands.

I saw the kid return to his empty bench. He noticed that his stuff was missing and he saw me and started to make a scene. 'Heeeeyyyyyyy! What the hell are you doing, man?' he whined loudly.

On the other side of the field Security had finally cottoned on to the fact that I wasn't part of the scheduled entertainment. Three or four burly men in blue uniforms started running straight towards me. I knew I had to act fast or not at all, but I couldn't think of anything else to say.

'The Mat sat on the Cat!' I hollered. 'The Mat sat on the Cat!'

The crowd erupted into a roar of approval and hysterical laughter, and for some reason that escapes me, I realised they were enjoying the spectacle. I found myself strangely excited by their show of fanatical support. I felt bullet-proof, invincible. People were finally listening.

I managed to dodge the first two Security guys and broke into a sprint across the field. One of them grabbed my jacket briefly but I shook him off and continued to bellow into the megaphone.

'The Mat sat on the Cat!' I yelled over and over. 'The Mat sat on the Caaattttttt!'

I couldn't elude these guys forever, though, and I knew it. The third guard tackled me, hitting me viciously from behind. The megaphone and lion's head went whistling through the air and I was thrown to the ground. The other brutes landed on me heavily, one by one, piling on top of me like angry lemmings. They pinned me to the turf and handcuffed me. The crowd continued to cheer me on even as I was being led, a bit too forcefully I thought, from the field amid thousands of approving onlookers. But had I delivered the warning, I wondered? Had I gotten the message across?

Then, almost as if it were all for nothing, just when it seemed that my display was viewed as nothing more than an entertaining but mindless show of dissent, the crowd started to chant. It was only a few of them at first, but then it really caught on. 'The Mat sat on the Cat!' they cried in unison. 'The Mat sat on the Cat!'

Their recitation of my mantra, to my ears, was like a revelation. It was a beautiful and sacred thing. I had succeeded in my mission. The Cats of the world would finally stand a chance against the scourge of every homicidal Door Mat in existence. Thanks to me, the rebellion had finally begun.

'Do you know what happened to my Mat?' I asked the brute who had handcuffed me.

'Don't be a smart arse!' he croaked meanly.

'No, I'm serious,' I insisted. 'It's very important!'

Then, as I was being most impolitely shoved inside the back of a squad car, he asked me something that I had to think about for a moment before I answered.

'Who the hell do you think you are?' he grunted.

'Me?' I asked in surprise. I was quite pleased that he was showing an interest. Grinning triumphantly from ear to ear I replied, 'I'm a Writer.'

The Wild and Unpredictable Sea

Gladys Slattery surges down a white hallway. Propelled by a sense of urgency, she pushes the elderly gentleman she knows only as Captain, in his rickety wheelchair. Their mission is simple: get to the Recreation and Gaming Parlour as soon as possible. Captain hollers out directions to Gladys as they go, navigating their way through the labyrinthine web of nerve like passageways that spread throughout the Moralpanik Ministry Asylum. There is a pungent stench in the air. It is as if someone vomited bleach into an over-chlorinated swimming pool and then painted the walls and floors with it.

'Thank you for this,' Gladys says. She struggles to control her gag reflex, puffing and slightly out of breath from their manic pace.

'That's perfectly fine, Gladys,' Captain replies. 'I'd much rather be in your capable hands than with one of the nurses. I just hope we're not too late,' he says gallantly, yet also hinting at their ominous predicament.

When Gladys arrived back at the Moralpanik Ministry Asylum, after leaving her son in the care of the grease-painted reptilian staff, she was shocked to discover they had discharged him from his room. To her surprise, Captain was waiting for her outside the empty padded cell that had held Joseph since his arrival. This time Captain was alone, without a nurse hovering over his pockmarked neck with a needle and glistening black syringe. He also seemed keen to help her. Ever since Gladys and Captain met in that broken elevator, he has become a recurrent and friendly face in the Asylum. Nobody else has been as warm and generous with their time as the Captain has. He has endeared himself to Gladys Slattery most admirably.

'They keep changing the visiting hours, Captain,' she says to him earnestly. 'Last night they barely gave me fifteen minutes with my son and I was told I should leave. When I made a fuss, they practically escorted me off the premises. They said they would look after him. At first, I could stay for an hour. It keeps changing every visit. Why did the staff let Joseph out of isolation without telling me? His head wound is still not healed and he doesn't belong here and...' Gladys says, her voice trailing off in confusion and worry.

'He really should have been sent up to the Superhero Ward straight away. That's where Joseph belongs, if anywhere. If I'm correct, they will have given him his dose of medication without water and told him that if he takes it to the Recreation and Gaming Parlour, he can exchange it for his precious little red cape. But that's just an educated guess, Gladys. They will tell all sorts of insidious lies to get the patients to play the Medication Mind-Blitz Machines. Once someone is on them for even a short while they're hooked. If we're lucky we might catch him before it's too late,' Captain says, speaking like a man on an important mission who is used to being on such esteemed and good-willed expeditions. Yes, a man who genuinely cares about the patients in the asylum; a man who stays on even though he can leave any time he wishes.

'Why are these machines so dangerous, Captain?' Gladys asks as they wind through the hallways. 'It seems awfully inappropriate to subject patients to something that is clearly bad for their mental health.'

Captain places his hands on the wheels of his chair to pause their journey. They are at another intersection interspersed with doors on all sides.

He swings himself around to face Gladys, temporarily lost in the asylum hallways; the paradox of the machines is unravelling in his mind. He suddenly seems eager to be still for a moment...to confide in her. 'They want to suck the hope out of people, to zombify them, make them dependant on the machines,' he says sadly, lowering his voice.

Yet in Captain's tone there is also an unmistakable enthusiasm for the subject that seems, despite the urgency of their mission, to be intensifying. Gladys tries to hurry him along, but Captain seems overly preoccupied with his own thoughts for the moment.

'Their official line…' he continues bitterly and somewhat unabated, 'is that the machines will inspire a sense of competitive gain and a motivation the patients need to be rehabilitated, qualities they say will help them in the outside world. But it's all hogwash, Gladys,' Captain gushes. 'Only by promising impossibilities and offering glimmers of trivial hope can they more fully snatch it all away from us forever. If the patients here would only take their specific dosage of medication, if they could only be satisfied that it can sometimes help them to cope with their problems, the Machines would be redundant. But no, Gladys, we gamble it all away on hypnotic empty promises and an insidious hunger for victory over machines that are programmed to destroy people's hopes. These machines, small deaths they offer, Gladys…interspersed by random, although sometimes quite sizeable wins. But whenever a hoard of shiny pills comes out of those damnable machines, it is inevitably put back in them…only tenfold. And it all seems to be an act of free will on the part of the addict, but it most certainly isn't! No, the machine's primary function is to be fed. The addict believes they will be rewarded for feeding the beast, while also feeding their own inexplicable need to suffer. The addict yearns for a symbiotic relationship with the beast, but when an addict receives that reward it only makes them more dependent…and so hungry, Gladys… I was an addict myself, you know. It is hard to describe the agony of withdrawal and loss, the tumultuous horror and the panic and devastation of pissing it all away again and again, without remembering the high: the wonder of the feast, the wins, the dance with the Demon, the mini-jackpot, the ludicrous but exquisite special feature that almost was but then just wasn't! It's so futile, Gladys. It's so soul-destroying to lose and lose and lose, and then, when that delicious small victory does happen, to put all those bounteous treasures – those beautiful glimmering shiny little pills that promise sanity and redemption – right back into the slavering mouth of the machine. More, more, more! I used to cry, Gladys,' Captain rants. He is almost frothing at the mouth now. 'But the nothingness of our mad desire to conquer the machine is never enough!' he hollers.

Captain pauses, catching the glimpse of fear and discomfort in Gladys's eyes at his rabid portrayal of addiction, and he again tries to calm himself. 'I'm so sorry, Gladys,' he says, realising he has gone too far. 'I don't mean to unnecessarily alarm you. We must keep going. If Joseph has been playing them for even a few hours, you will find it terribly difficult to reach him,' Captain says, sounding every bit like a reformed junkie and a gentleman who knows his way around the asylum and the mysterious machines.

Captain is not only charming and gregarious, thinks Gladys, but he seems to truly, passionately care. Unfortunately, his rambling spiel, although in equal measure enlightening and horrifying, has brought their expedition to a temporary standstill.

'Which way now, Captain?' Gladys stresses, hoping to keep moving. Captain's words have made her feel even more eager to get to Joseph now before he's lost to her forever.

'Down this way,' he shouts, gesturing to the right like a military leader ordering an army to charge. 'If you listen carefully, you can hear them,' he says.

Gladys powers the chair to the right, and the rubber wheels squeal against the tiles. She can hear something as they get closer. The sound is a merry clatter of synthetic beeps, alarms, bells and banal musical interludes. She can hear the groaning mechanical voices of the machines and perhaps, Gladys thinks…perhaps even the unconscious and miserable hum of despondent, zombified patients. Is that what she can hear, the small deaths that Captain spoke of?

'Oh, my poor Joseph…' she frets. 'What shall we do when we get there, Captain?' she asks in distress.

'We need to be very careful not to make a scene, my dear. Lest the nurses throw me into solitary confinement and you are thrown out of here for good. And believe me, they will react harshly if provoked. The nurses are a nasty breed and, as you've seen, they are armed. If Joseph is playing a Mind-Blitz Machine, and it is quite possible, Gladys, you must approach him with caution. No sudden movements. Hug him from behind, whisper in his ear that you'd like him to come for a walk… If you can coax him away, I'll figure out the rest from there,' Captain says, slowing the chair with his hands as they reach a corner where the noises and lights of the parlour are at last manifest.

'You wander in before me. Try to look curious, inquisitive, as if you are entering a parlour of delights and not the dreaded pit of the demonic and the damned. See if you can spot him,' he says. 'I'm considered somewhat of a troublemaker by the staff here and my presence may hinder your attempts at intervention. It will be less conspicuous if we enter the parlour separately,' the Captain whispers conspiratorially.

'Can you get around on your own, I mean…in that chair of yours,' Gladys asks in concern.

'My arms aren't what they used to be but I can manoeuvre quite well on my own. Stamina can be a problem, but I'll be fine. If they escort me off, I'm afraid you'll be on your own, but I hope to God it doesn't come to that. Good luck, my dear lady, and please do be careful. Joseph may not want to move. In fact, he may not be able to.'

Before Gladys Slattery can ask what Captain means by this last remark, her legs have already carried her through the doors of the Recreation and Gaming Parlour, propelled by urgency and a mother's instinct to save her wayward son from the dreaded clutches of the Medication Mind-Blitz Machines.

Gladys is immediately struck by the overwhelming glitz and the sleek high-tech ambience of the room. She feels dizzy, as if the room is revolving around her. It seems that everything in the parlour but the poor despondent patients is pulsating like a psychedelic carousel. Many of them are strapped to the Mind-Blitz Machines with leather belts and statically charged coloured wires. There are hundreds of whizzing, whirring machines, commanding every patient's complete focus. Their fingers mindlessly tap on the array of keys at their disposal repetitively and with little change in pace or emphasis. The effect is one of mind numbing, unchanging hypnotic motion. Tap, tap, tap, tap, they go, on and on like brain-fried writers on computer keyboards pressing the same key for an eternity. There is little expression or change on their faces, not even when a machine drops a clatter of shiny psychotropic pills in the tray at their knee level, or as they methodically place the pills, one by one by one, back in the mouth of their machine. The machines themselves are aligned in winding rows in the centre of the parlour and line the vast mirrored walls. The mirrors give the impression that the room and all its lights and the stooped, almost lifeless figures, stretch infinitely in all directions. Repeated, cloned and warped in a disturbing and inescapable forever-ness that defies any conception of logic.

Once Gladys has found her balance, she wanders in small calculated steps towards a nearby counter occupied by two reptilian nurses. She scans the seated patients for any sign of her son as she goes.

'Excuse me,' Gladys says politely to one of the nurses, 'but I'm looking for my son Joseph.'

'What?' the nurse snaps back rudely.

'I'm looking for Joseph Slattery. I thought he might be here. I'm his mother, Gladys.'

'And why would you be doing that?' the nurse says coldly. Her black orbed snake eyes glare and expand, immediately swallowing what feels to Gladys like all the light and hope from the room.

'Because I want to see him?' Gladys guesses timidly, hoping it is an appropriate answer.

'I'm ssssure he'ssss findable, madame. Do you not possesssss eyessss and legssss?' she hisses.

'Of course, um…' Gladys falters nervously.

'Well, I suggessst that you ussse them,' the nurse says, waving Gladys away with her hand and getting back to the task of sorting through a tray of shiny little pills and placing them in white waxen cups.

Gladys turns to see an empty wheelchair in the middle of the carpeted walkway between the machines. To her horror, Captain has clawed his way out of his chair and is attempting to climb up onto the seat of one of the machines using his arms.

She scuttles up behind him as he is halfway up. 'Captain!' she gasps, 'What are you doing?'

'Help me up please, nurse,' he says, with his eyes glued to the flashing screen.

Without questioning him further, Gladys offers him a bewildered hand to get seated.

'Captain?' Gladys inquires again, now quite alarmed by this sudden turn of events.

But Captain does not reply. When he has positioned himself comfortably on the seat, he rubs his hands together in satisfied glee and chuckles to himself mischievously. Then, as if he is greeting an old foe he says, 'Well, helllllooooo there, Demon!'

Two red wires with little circular pads on the ends suddenly shoot out from the sides of the machine and hover ominously over his temples.

'Are you ready to ride the wild and unpredictable sea?' the Machine purrs slyly.

'Aye, aye, that I am, Demon!' the Captain says, sounding like a cartoon approximation of a seafaring adventurer or perhaps, thinks Gladys, the about to be jolly-rogered Captain of a computerised pirate ship.

She takes a step back, wondering what happened to the gallant gentleman of five minutes ago.

'Do you have gold upon you, Sailor?' the Machine asks, its wires still poised over the sides of his skull like two snakes poised to strike.

'Aye, aye, Demon, that I do.'

Captain eagerly rummages through his pockets and hastily

retrieves a handful of multi-hued medication. As he begins slotting the pills into the mouth of the machine, the wired pads latch onto his temples and burrow into his skin. They begin to throb and grind like sucker fish as the screen bubbles into life and dozens of reels with images of sharks, numbers, anchors and treasure chests centre themselves on the screen. Captain presses a yellow lit button and the reels spin, each one clicking into place as if in random sequence. Yet when they have ceased spinning nothing happens. There is no conjoined sequence of similar images to see. No win. No victory. Captain begins to literally drool on himself. His shoulders slump forward and his eyes glaze over. He continues to press the button with the same results, and his hand begins to shake as it prods at the button's fading light.

'Need more gold, I do, aye, aye, Captain, ohhhhhh, no, no, no…' he begins to blabber sadly as his credit quickly disappears, falling to absolute zero in two last shaky prods.

'Nurse? Nurse?' Captain says, turning to Gladys, almost as if in a delirium. 'Need me pills, I do, aye…' he trails off miserably, as if defeated.

Gladys shakes him by the shoulders vigorously. 'Captain?' she says in vain. 'Captain? I need your help to find Joseph. Please help me.'

Captain ignores her. He turns back to the screen and continues to press the button. But it is futile. The screen begins to fade but the wires and suckered pads stay in place on the sides of his head, slurping hungrily on his cerebrum.

Prod, prod, prod…

Tap, tap, tap…

Still, nothing happens. The machine does not respond. Captain just keeps on pressing the same button anyway.

There is suddenly an excited shout of victory from the other side of the room. 'Woooohooooooooo!' someone yells.

To Gladys, the enthusiastic yelp is immediately familiar. It must be Joseph.

The sound is followed by the drawled murmurs of suddenly intrigued and alert patients, and the unmistakable clattering of a flood of pills spewing into the tray of a Mind-Blitz Machine.

Even Captain snaps out of his delirium. He turns to Gladys and, the fog that clouded his eyes abruptly parts. He says, 'Gladys! Joseph is here. He just hit the mini-jackpot!'

Captain tears at the wired pads attached to his temples, but they are stubborn and it takes all his strength to rip them off. He recklessly throws himself from the stool onto the carpeted floor near his wheelchair with a giant sprawling thud.

Gladys leaves him there and races around the row of machines towards the origin of the noise. When she reaches the far corner of the parlour, she sees Joseph. He has leapt up from the machine he was playing and is dancing around in circles, joyously pretending he is flying. He dips and twirls like a wannabe superhero engaged in the initial stages of an attack of gleeful epilepsy, grinning maniacally. He makes exaggerated whooshing sounds in full view of the spellbound patients on the surrounding machines. The nursing staff gave him back his little red cape and he is wearing it with pride and suitably deranged aplomb. The only other stitches of clothing on him are the luminous, skin tight red bathers Gladys gave him to replace the nappy he initially wore in solitary confinement.

'Joseph!' she calls out emphatically, her voice cutting like a scythe through the commotion.

Joseph suddenly pauses, ending his frantic dance. He looks up and across the room, recognising his mother immediately. 'Mummy!' he calls back excitedly. 'Look, I won!'

Gladys notices that the nurses have moved from behind their counter and are approaching Joseph. One of them is holding a large, glistening black needle. Joseph notices them too, and he seems to realise he is in some form of imminent danger. In his mind, the nurses are approaching to take his precious red cape off him again, and Joseph is having none of it.

Thinking quickly, he reaches into the overflowing tray of pills and scoops them up into his hands. 'Woooohooooo!' he yelps again and throws the shiny psychotropic pills high into the air above his head.

They rain down on the surrounding patients like glimmering hailstones and scatter all over the carpeted floor. Before the nurses can reach him, patients from all over the room have leapt from their machines and are clawing across the floor, competing to collect as many of the fallen medication units as possible. Soon there are dozens of them pawing at the ground around Joseph's feet.

'Good boy, Joseph!' Gladys shouts encouragingly, noticing that the diversion is working perfectly. The nurses have paused and are looking around the room in panic. They cannot get to Joseph now.

'Do it again, Joseph!' Gladys shouts again.

Joseph continues to scoop more and more pills into his hands and throw them high into the air. He too has realised the diversion is succeeding. More and more patients have now abandoned their machines, now clear eyed and full of desperate vigour and competitive motion. They gather the pills, jostling and scrambling for more precious gold to feed their insatiable machines.

The Captain, who has somehow managed to claw his way back into his wheelchair, suddenly rolls up beside Gladys. He is no longer under the spell of his machine. There is fire in his eyes. He stares longingly at the rabble of patients and the scattered ocean of fallen and still falling medication rain. 'You have to get Joseph out of here, Gladys,' Captain says. 'And make it fast!'

'Will they let us out of the gate?' Gladys asks in panic.

'The exit will still be accessible. Just swipe your card and act calm. Make sure Joseph stays a few metres behind you so the main camera doesn't recognise him. If he's quick, he'll be able to follow you through. The nurses at the entrance will be confused by what's going on here in the gaming parlour, so hopefully they won't be expecting it. They'll have other concerns. They're in crowd control mode now, but it won't last. Make a run for it while you can. I'll hold them off.'

'Joseph!' Gladys calls out. 'Come with me!'

Joseph throws one more handful of pills in the direction of the nurses and then begins stepping through the seething throng at his feet. He walks over the backs of some of the other patients and tramples on quite a few limbs on his way to his mother.

The nurses are now completely baffled; they don't know what to do to control the clearly out-of-control rabble. As if on cue, three white-coated male security staff armed with charged electrical prods enter from the other side of the parlour and begin brutally zapping the patients one by one, leaving their unfortunate victims twitching in agony, writhing on the floor like dying cockroaches. But there are far too many for them to handle and the rebellion continues.

When Joseph reaches his mother, they embrace.

Gladys sobs in relief and drags Joseph out through the parlour doors. 'Thank you, Captain,' she says on her way.

'That's perfectly all right, Gladys,' Captain calls out gallantly, as if he is the esteemed and valiant hero of some fantastical war. 'I'm just glad to be of service! Now run, both of you!'

As Gladys and Joseph hastily embark on their escape, the Captain notices a few pills that have rolled under his wheelchair. Looking around cautiously to be certain that no one is looking, he stoops down and retrieves them, stuffing them into his pockets. Edging forwards in his chair, one by one by one, he collects still more. The Captain briefly contemplates putting one into his mouth but decides against it. No, he'll need them for later, when he once more boards his majestic ship to sail the Wild and Unpredictable Sea.

*

Fifteen minutes later, Gladys and her Super-Duper-Man son Joseph are gunning along the Palpitation Motorway in her old, green, rust-bucket Beamer. Joseph is grinning like a defiant loon, still mesmerised by the thrill of their narrow escape and his victorious battle over the machine. Gladys is still trying to control her irregular breathing, the panicked aftermath of an intensely dramatic series of scenes that she can barely believe happened at all. She drives her old car like a woman possessed, still convinced they may have been followed and might be caught, and her poor son Joseph locked up for good. But there is also a sense of adrenalised purpose to her acceleration, as if she has just accomplished the impossible; rescuing her beloved son from the dreaded clutches of the Moralpanik Ministry Asylum and its sadistic reptilian staff. It was a most inhospitable and hostile hospital if there ever was one, she thinks.

'Are we going to see Mary?' Joseph asks hopefully, 'We're pregnant you know… I want to see my Mary, Mum.'

'No, Joseph, we're going home for now,' Gladys says calmly.

'Is it my birthday today?' her son asks, with a bewildered sense of wonderment in his tone.

'Yes, Joseph, it is indeed…' Gladys replies warmly, smiling through what are now tears, 'and I'm going to bake you the best birthday cake you've ever had.'

Joseph suddenly sticks his head out of the car window and begins to raucously sing. 'Happy birthday too meeee!' he chortles loudly, performing his birthday song in a wavering baritone to everyone and anyone who might conceivably be listening.

The tears in Gladys Slattery's eyes are streaming down her cheeks in vast torrents now. Yet for some unfathomable reason not even she understands, she cannot stop smiling.

The Night Inside the Day

My Papa is a dead man but he's more alive than most. Some people have a way of living on, well after the foul heart desists. My Papa is a dead man but he's more alive than me.

I move towards an impossible horizon. The imaginary line keeps pace with me. Every one of my steps is matched by its own. My days bleed into nights, the seasons into shame; a strange panic descends upon my dreams like a fog.

Every morning is the same. I awake to the ghostly rhythm of my Papa's snoring. The sleep in my eye's coils around the blurry vision that revealed itself to me in my slumber. I crawl from beneath a mountain of linen, ever towards the crack of light that lingers between the white folds of sheet and the outside world.

I sip black coffee and devour cigarettes. The smoke curls and shimmers, dancing for me in the air. Patterns form and then dissipate, like visions in passing clouds. I suspect there is a divine logic to their permutations, but it eludes me. They are gone before I can understand them, replaced by other ripples and other contorted faces.

I flick through the *Moralpanik Daily News*, peeling back the pages with a ritual curiosity. An article on the second page sparks my interest. It details the police's ongoing search for a missing priest. Ah yes, another one. For some reason, they just keep going missing. There is a small photograph of the man. Strange, something about his face strikes me as familiar. I am perplexed. Perhaps I have passed him in the local park on my way to the bus stop? I peruse the article. It ends with a distraught plea from a small rabble of the priest's devoted parishioners asking for anyone who may have seen him to please notify the police.

I am suddenly nauseous…vision blurring…stumbling over to the telephone…and I…pick up the receiver…dial a number…ringing… ringing…

Perry is five. One day Perry will be six, but my Papa he does say I will be five forever. My face is pale with rosy cheeks, Mumma did tell me so. But inside the closet it is so very, very dark, the night inside the day. If Papa does be pleased with me, I do sleep in my bedroom, so I do try to please my Papa. But Papa is coming to punish Perry. Perry has been bad…sssshhhhh, don't make a sound. Footsteps in the hall, growing louder coming closer beating faster…sssshhhh, listen. Hands opening the closet, hands reaching for Perry…

Papa is here.

My Papa is a dead man. I keep his empty wheelchair by the bed.

After the stroke, my Papa used the chair to get around the house. His pride took a fall, but his mind continued to possess the fury of the righteous faithful. The hardest thing for my Papa was that the stroke had left him physically dependent on me, his only son. And Papa was stubborn. He would often refuse my help, hurling abuse at me for driving him to an early grave. He would rather put up with the mess in his pants than admit that he couldn't do it on his own. My Papa felt betrayed by God, yet he remained zealous and violently prayerful to the last. I was his cross to bear, he would say; I was the thorn in his side. I cared for him as best I could in those final years, suffering his endless taunts and bitter tirades like a beaten dog, weary from the constant rattle of sadistic guilt.

Papa was tormented by visions of the Serpent. His head was consumed with unearthly voices. He swore that my mother, who took her own life when I was only four, was the origin of these voices. He struggled with her threats long into the night, clamping his hands over his ears and bellowing prayers into the emptiness. According to Papa, my mother had made an unholy pact with the Serpent, to pollute his faith and wither his mortal coil. She haunted the corridors of his conscience like a jackal, persistently gnawing at his feeble corpse and threatening to drag it into hell. At times, Papa was convinced that I was trying to poison him, and that my deceased mother had put me up to it.

My Papa is a dead man, but sometimes I can hear the wheels of his chair squealing across the cold vinyl floor of the kitchen. I know that these sounds are merely echoes, shadows of the way I wish to remember him: a broken man.

But he wasn't always like that. There was a time I can remember, when I was just a small boy, when my Papa possessed the conviction of his God, and the guile of the Serpent.

My Papa oh my Papa and his silver crucifix much too close. It is the symbol where I do lay my eyes. I am afraid to move them from the little Jesus man in Papa's chest hair, heaving with each breath, flailing in the unbearable eternity between each second.

'Lord forgive me,' I do hear him moan. Hands warm and urgent on my limbs they do stroke smack squeeze Oh suck scratch spank bite push crush hush hussshhh…sssshhhh…

Papa oh my Papa, your tongue grinding into the back of my neck, your arm under my ribcage, your invisible mouth grunting to God.

'Tis the Serpent who guides my hand thus,' Papa does say. He does always be tempted into sin by the Serpent. 'This closet is the Desert and you are the Serpent,' Papa does say. 'You must tempt me into sin and I must sin because I am a man.'

Other times he does say different. 'I am the Serpent and you are the man.'

If I am a filthy bad one and I cry for my Mumma, he does say, 'I am Jesus and you are the Serpent, and I shall punish you.'

I stare into the bathroom mirror and strain to see past the filth. I am crucified with toothbrushes, bleeding hair gel from the wounds in my hands and feet. Riveted to the mirror with shards of foggy glass. Toothpaste oozes from the hole in my side, emerging lasciviously, like a pasty white worm. I thrill at the cold burning sensation it leaves on my stomach. Ribs hungrily feasting on the skin of my chest. Cheek bones sharp and skeletal white.

I am forever altered, estranged from all other characters in this, the bleakest of dreamscapes.

Papa Dilworth preached his gospel from the streets, sometimes setting up his mobile mission on the corner outside the local grocery store. It was there that he bellowed his message of conditional love and eternal damnation to his flock of passers-by. On occasion he would allow me to attend, dressing me in an oversized altar-boy robe and having me hold his tattered Bible as he read from it. I felt proud to be a part of my Papa's street church, but it frightened me to observe the differences in him. At times I felt accepted and loved, convincing myself that God had forgiven me for my filth. But it never lasted. I was on display, my Papa playing the proud and loving father and the passionate disciplinarian, and I the prodigal son. Yet only when I appeased his demons was I welcomed back into the fold.

Pleasing my Papa was no easy task, for it required appealing to his sense of pride. To survive the Serpent's wrath, I had to worship the Serpent as God. To appease God, I had to play the sacrificial lamb. The only constant was complete subservience to the whims of his imagination, and the erratic manifestations of his desire. I strived to develop characters that would help me to stay in my Papa's favour. I loved my Papa but I knew that I didn't deserve his love. And in time my Papa's manipulations became my own, infecting my prayers with confused logic and desperation. I slowly began to realise, even at a very young age, that there was more than one Papa.

Dear God, I been speaking to the Serpent…my Papa…my God…and he does say I been bad but I do swear I been good. If Perry has been a good one, how does Papa know the Serpent is not a fibber? My Papa oh my Papa did say that you can see me when I am bad, but he did also say that you and the Serpent cannot see me in the closet…not when Papa does be in here with me anyway…but I do hope you do hear me… I do be in here cos I been filthy…again and again I do be dirty and locked away an' my Papa he does say I will never learn…but I can learn to be good I can… I can… Clean I will be…but Papa knows and Papa sees and Papa punishes…but

During Preacher Dilworth's street corner services, his manner would swing wildly and without warning. From moral saviour to prophet of damnation, the pendulum's erratic motion often left his meagre audiences humbled, exhausted and sometimes volatile. His talent for telling intimate and amusing stories could quite easily segue into the scathing parables of a crazed evangelical. The unpredictable nature of his sermonising was often too overwhelming for the locals, and people would cross the street to avoid him. Despite this, the locals begrudgingly respected him, for his overwhelming dedication to the Word of God, and simply by the sheer force of his personality. He made it his business to call out to people by name, interrupting his sermons to wish those who passed by either a jovial blessing or to warn them of the wayward paths of sin.

Preacher Dilworth had not attended the seminary. His school grades weren't good enough. He learnt the particulars of his vocation from *The Holy Babble* and a copy of Father Daniel Ribach's *Walk with the Lord: A Preacher's Guide to the Holy Life*. He conducted his services with ritual determination, turning bottles of Stone's green ginger wine and loaves of Limey's toasting bread into the flesh and blood of his Christ. Not many folks regularly attended these rituals, mostly just street bums and homeless kids looking for some food and a mouthful of wine.

Preacher Dilworth did, however, have a small group of dedicated parishioners. Certain families, those too poor and proud to attend the local church, remained loyal to his teachings. The Pinkelbys, Robert and Judith and their five young children, attended at least twice a week. They honoured Preacher Dilworth and his teachings with an almost religious fanaticism. He was their moral guardian and good shepherd.

Preacher Dilworth utilised the stories of *The Holy Babble* to throttle and bewilder his congregation, randomly snatching phrases from Revelations or Deuteronomy and weaving them into what were often wildly unpredictable sermons. Occasionally he would coax some local shoppers into participating in his street corner service, but not very often. Most of the religious folks in the area considered him to be operating outside of the church. An old school radical without the refinement or training of the local minister, Father Robert Weavilby.

Weavilby drove a white Volvo and often made house calls to his parishioners, for morning teas smattered with idle gossip, cups of Tetley tea and Iced Vovo biscuits. Preacher Dilworth warned his audiences of the evils of Father Weavilby, branding him a heathen and messenger of the Serpent. Besides, Papa was convinced Father Weavilby was bedding a large proportion of his female congregation.

lock click shut close rape trap snap crack

I know Papa, I know the Serpent is the fiend, the hurt. Oh, Papa stop, stop it, I can still feel you in me, in me like a dirty spider. Perry is forever pleading with the hairy spider to stop it. But quietly, silently, oh yes Papa he does love my mouth but only when it is a quiet mouth. Papa still too tightly holding my bruised arms, still trapped in the shadows, loving me and punishing me, still too trapped in his arms to take flight and run and run and my cheeks streaked with the Serpents tears. Begging to be buried in my Mumma's bosom.

'Mumma is dead, child. The Serpent took her from us.'

'But I did seen her, Papa, I seen her through the crack in the closet.'

'Mumma is in hell, child. Your Mumma didn't love you.'

But I did know Mumma was there. Lightly kiss my bruises, Mumma, ah yes hold me, brush your lips across my forehead. Ah like that, Mumma yes, quivering with me in your arms your bosom muffling my cries.

'Mumma is dead, child. The Serpent took her away,' Papa does say.

But I do know she would never leave me. My Mumma does know Papa touches me. Spied her through the crack in the door I did, watching the locked closet with a nervous crease in her brow. Head ever so slightly tilted, ever listening for a whimper from my bitten lips. But she never does come too close, my Mumma. For she knows, knows it is God's retribution for my badness, my unforgivable filth, the Serpent working through my Papa, punishing me for all my dirtiness and sin. Bruises and Papa bleeding me for being a naughty child, and I truly am a bad one, Papa he does tell me so.

Perry is frightened, Mumma, the shadows they do grunt and groan, but quietly oh so silently, Mumma. You will hear them if you do listen closely. I am leaving the door slightly ajar and waiting patiently for you to come visit me.

My Papa is a dead man. He is the hairy spider in my blood.

Sometimes I venture into my Papa's old bedroom and stare at the closet. I don't know why. I can stare into it for hours, in disturbed awe, almost as if I expect to see something, someone. Like a small boy chewing his bottom lip, waiting for his father, or a spot of dry blood seeping into the knotted wood, masked by the shadows. And sometimes, I feel compelled to get inside and shut the doors behind me. I do not understand the impulse, nor the morbid fascination it inspires in me.

But I know that it is wrong.

All that I am is wrong.

Every morning I travel to work on the bus, eyes fixed on a place between my shoes and the back of a stranger's head. At the office I go to great lengths to avoid conversation, though if I must, I will comment on the weather. Hot, isn't it? Yes, a bit of rain would be good. Bit nippy out. Have you noticed that the winters seem to be getting colder? Is it humid or am I just imagining it?

When asked about my weekend, I manufacture elaborate stories about friends I do not have and places that I have never been. The truth is too revealing, and I doubt my colleagues would understand.

I travel home from work to an empty house, my childhood home. It has become my new closet, resounding with the timeless echoes of my Papa's bedside bell. The television is always on, but there is no aerial, no discernible picture and no sound. I derive comfort from its muffled glow.

It is always there, waiting for me, in the corner of my eye.

Papa the Spider does devour me, eats me up in the fairy tales. Papa does tell them to me, tells me so majestic and grand does Papa. I do be Hansel and Gretel and Papa does be the Witch. Papa tells me how the naughty children do be eaten up by the Witch for not fearing the Serpent. And I do get swallowed up by the Wolf when I be Little Red-Riding Hood. My Papa does do the telling and I do listen.

But oh my…

How the worm it does turn.

Now I am the teller…and YOU are the listener.

LITTLE MISSY MUFFET SHE DID SAT IN A CLOSET, EATING UP HER CURDS AND HER WHEYS. BUT ALONG CAME A HAIRY SPIDER AND DID SNEAKED UP BEHIND HER AND DID TEACH NAUGHTY MISS MUFFET TO PRAY.

I do clap at the end of Papa's telling and Papa he does eat me up.

All the while my lips I am biting.

My Papa is a dead man. I am the terror in the wind.

Warning. There is an underside to every tapestry, a studied motion in every performance. Some secrets were never meant to be shared. It is better that way. Trust me. If I am anything, I am a witness to your spiritual descent. And it is indeed a glorious journey, a practised metaphor for the places that you hide, inside the closet, in the darkest hole, in the fear that wells up inside you, like endless oceans in pretty blue eyes.

It is the secret evolution of blood, father to son, spider to web spun.

My Papa is a dead man. But I do love him still.

I stare through the grey static that blinds the television eye. Reeling through the images in my head, my Papa's last breath playing over and over like a schizoid mirage; a sinister vision I can neither stop nor reject, scanning for something, a thought, a word, something that might answer the echoes. One frame recurs with eerie clarity. I try to block it out, ignore it. Shake it from my ears. But it is too strong.

I see my hands, trembling in the air in front of my face, gripping a set of marble black rosary beads. I stroke their sparkling length with quickening anticipation, my fingers pulse with the Serpent's blood, my vision shifts in and out of focus. My Papa is slumped in his wheelchair by the bed. He stares at the crucifix on the wall, gibbering on and on as if engaged in conversation with the wooden Christ. I approach slowly, from behind, but all the while I am thinking I want him to see my face. I want to be the last thing he sees, right before the cruel darkness steals his…

No.

I cannot…I will not let…IT, engulf ME…but the cold rage it does spill over from somewhere secret far behind my eyes and the fall of angels wakes my hands to violence…my Papa oh my Papa…screaming now and he's cackling with laughter…or is he begging for me to stop? I drag him from the wheelchair to the bedroom to the closet by his hair and force him inside…kicking and screaming and begging…and I can't I WILL NOT LET IT ENGULF ME…the dirty spider in my blood spills out of the closet so I lash out and smash and fuck and bruise the spider…furiously forcing fucking smashing crushing the closet doors closed on the dirty spider's head…over and over and over…he cries for mercy begs for it to stop to stop and I finally get the doors to close on the spider and I'm leaping out of the shadows and taking IT back…days pass like storm clouds over an imaginary night sky and the desperate scratching of fingernails on wood soon ceases altogether…the feeble whimpering of the dying spider recedes…like pitiful shadows trapped in a locked closet…

Quiet…ssssshhhhh… Perry is coming, yes, he is… Papa?… Papa? Perry is here.

Silence.

My Papa is alive. He lives within my head. Some folks have a way of living on, well after the foul heart desists. Men, women and children disappear all the time. And priests… Ah yes, one by one by one they disappear, these so-called men of the cloth. But there are no funerals, and no bodies are ever found. Missing posters are scraped from store windows like dead skin, torn from trees to make room for new nightmares, and new reasons for searching. Sometimes I recognise a name, like a character in someone else's dream, or a series of thoughts in somebody else's head. But I almost always recognise their faces, their silent protestations. I can almost taste their sweet and tearful prayers. But most of all, I see the unmistakable reflection of the Serpent in their eyes.

And finally, I know, as their silent terror grips me, that I am not alone.

www.ingramcontent.com/pod-product-compliance
Lightning Source LLC
Chambersburg PA
CBHW020334110726
47898CB00003B/873